BITTER HOUSE

KIERSTEN MODGLIN

KIERSTEN
MODGLIN
The Last Notes

Cover Design by Kiersten Modglin
Copy Editing by Three Owls Editing
Proofreading by My Brother's Editor
Formatting & Graphic Design by Kiersten Modglin
Author Photograph © Lisa Christianson

First Print and Electronic Edition: 2024
kierstenmodglinauthor.com

To family—
the one we're born into and
the one we build ourselves

OBITUARIES

'Devastated' — Family and City in Mourning Over the Passing of Beloved Matriarch, Vera Bitter

By: Jane LaRue

It's nearly impossible to live in the greater Nashville area without having heard the name Vera Bitter. Whether you met her through her extensive involvement in the art and music programs throughout the city, her annual gala, whose proceeds went directly toward funding food banks and toy drives every Christmas for underprivileged families; or perhaps her love for all things related to keeping our city green and beautiful, there's no doubt of the impact Vera Bitter had not only on our lives but on our great city.

Vera Evelyn Bitter, born Vera Evelyn Shuffle to her loving parents Troas and Hazel Shuffle on January 22, 1940, peacefully left the world Wednesday, February 7, 2024 at her home, lovingly called the Bitter House, here in Nashville, TN.

Vera had a lovely childhood, surrounded by her parents and seven brothers and sisters. Vera was ten years younger than her youngest brother and therefore often doted upon. The years of attention didn't cause Vera to lose sight of things outside of herself or to suffer from youngest-child syndrome. In fact, those who knew and loved her, like Cate Ellison, her next-door neighbor for the last thirty years, say Vera was 'kind and incomparably selfless' up until the very end.

From an early age, that selflessness was apparent as Vera displayed an unwavering determination to make a difference in the world. That desire, I'm told by those closest to her, would drive her throughout her very long and very full life.

When Vera was just twenty years old, she married her soulmate, Harold Bitter, and their love story became the stuff of legends and fairytales. The Bitters donated, participated in, and contributed to many of the city's greatest charitable causes.

The Bitters were blessed with two beautiful children, daughters they loved more than anything. They went on to have three grandchildren as well. Her family was the light of Vera's life. She and Harold were married for nearly thirty years before his sudden death in 1989.

After, Vera was married to Reginald Mosely for just seven months before their amicable divorce. In addition to her late husband, Vera is preceded in death by her parents; seven siblings; daughter, Christina; and son-in-law, Nathan

Lancaster. She is survived by her daughter Jennifer (Marcus) Nolan; grandchildren Bridget Lancaster, Zach Nolan and Jonah Nolan; as well as many friends.

Vera's passion for philanthropy empowered her to make a substantial impact on our community and, ultimately, the world. But Vera's greatest achievement and the thing she celebrated with the most joy will always be her family. The Bitter House was a place of shared love and laughter.

Vera Bitter's legacy is one of joy, compassion, and hard work, and it will forever be etched into Nashville's tapestry. The world is a little bit darker as of yesterday, when the family and close friends gathered to say goodbye to their beloved matriarch in a small, private ceremony at the Bitter House. Today and forever, we Nashvillians will remember her remarkable life—one filled with happiness, devotion, and an unwavering determination to make the world a better place. Her memory will forever be a guiding light to those lucky enough to know her, reminding us to live and lead with kindness above all else.

PART 1

CHAPTER ONE

BRIDGET

Bitter House. They got that about right, didn't they?

The house stands tall and desolate against the gray sky. Gray stone, white accents, with sharp angles and a fierce spire that towers several feet over the rest of the house. It's grand, spacious, and filled with sadness. Just...not for the reasons you think.

The newspaper lies in my front seat, the article about my grandmother and her amazing, selfless life face up.

The problem? *It's nothing but lies.*

Whoever wrote it clearly didn't know her at all, only what she wanted people to know. Which isn't unusual. No one knew her. Not even the children she raised. She wanted it that way. She was an enigma, a mystery. A giant question mark. A ghost that floated through that house and her life without ever making contact with anyone.

The funeral that was supposed to happen in a private ceremony yesterday—the one filled with close friends and family? It didn't exist. If it had, there would have been no one to come. No one who cared enough to say goodbye. In fact, as far as I know, Vera slipped out of the world without anyone noticing at all.

No one's lives will change in the slightest with her gone except for mine, and only out of a sense of obligation I don't fully understand.

When I received the news that my grandmother had passed away and that her house—Bitter House—was left to me, my feelings were conflicted at best.

On one hand, she raised me when she didn't have to, when I had nowhere else to go, but on the other, she was hardly warm. She was nothing like my mother, and I'm still trying to process my feelings about that.

When I graduated from high school, my grandmother all but dumped me on the porch steps of Bitter House with my bags and not so much as a goodbye, and I haven't heard from her since. Not once.

So finding out the family house was left to me is a surprise at the very least. I make my way down the winding drive, the tall, menacing manor in front of me, iron gate behind me.

As soon as the gate swung closed minutes ago, I felt my throat tighten, and I've yet to take a normal breath.

I pull the car to a stop at the end of the long, paved driveway and stare over at the house where I grew up. How many nights did I spend looking out that window right there, second one from the right on the top floor, wondering if there was really life outside of it? If I'd ever actually be able to get away from Bitter House and its influence.

If I'd known the reality of what life would look like on my own, I'm not sure I would've been in such a hurry to leave.

I check my phone and spot a text from my best friend, Ana.

> Hope you made it okay. I'll manage everything here until you get back, so don't worry. Let me know if you need anything, even if it's just to vent. Always here.

I type out a response quickly, wishing I could explain to her how strange this feels. I've tried to, of course, but it's not something you can put into words. Bitter House and the memories that come with it are heavy and thick, and wading through them is like swimming through batter. I'm not sure I know how I feel enough to understand it, let alone explain it to someone else, even to the person who knows me the best.

> Made it safely. Thanks for taking over work for me. If you need anything or get behind, I'm just a phone call away and can always work from here if I need to. Miss you already. I'll be back as soon as I can.

I step out of the car without gathering my bags. I'm not sure how long I'll be staying. Edna, the executor, said it was important that I come back before I make the decision whether to sell. If I do—which I really think I will, since I have no desire to ever live within these walls again—she wants me to see the place, go through whatever things I'd like to keep, and give her permission to donate the rest.

She didn't have to work too hard to convince me, though. Despite all of my conflicted feelings, regrets, and anger about the things that happened at Bitter House, it was still my home once. I'm, for lack of a better word, bitter about how things happened here. I'm angry and empty that Vera could cast me aside so easily, that she didn't think I even deserved an explanation as to why.

I hate that I ever trusted her, that I let myself rely on her. And, maybe more than anything else, I hate the fact that I still care. That despite the icy, detached way my grandmother raised me, it still matters to me that she was my grandmother. I need to come back here to say goodbye, to find closure on my own terms, maybe even to try to make sense of what seems impossible to understand.

I can't say goodbye to her without coming back to Bitter House, to the place where she shattered my already broken heart, and I have to say goodbye, even if it comes with a side of good riddance.

I cross the front lawn, walking on the grass and up the front steps. At the front door, I twist the key in the lock. The silver key had been included in the envelope Edna sent over, and it still feels foreign in my hand. I haven't attached it to my key ring, wanting to do nothing that might allow me to consider staying in this place, calling it home once again.

I push open the front door and step into the foyer, breathing in the familiar scent. It's lilac and dust—years of history and memories hidden within that smell—and it makes me feel sad and nostalgic and suffocated all at once.

With the door closed behind me, I tuck my hands into my pockets and stare around at a space that once felt like my entire world. A space that seemed to contract and expand based on my grandmother's moods, but despite its enormity, it never felt large enough to contain me.

She's everywhere in this place, though, even now that she's gone. Even as her body is currently being cremated and I know she'll never be anywhere else ever again, she's here. In the wallpaper she changed every few years. In the art she had hung on the wall, the curtains adorning the windows, and the light fixtures that remain permanently covered in dust.

In the study, which was always more decorative than functional, I sit down at her oversized desk, running my hands across the wooden top. There's so much here, I don't even know where to start when it comes to sorting through things.

I wanted to think I might be able to accomplish everything in just a few days, a week tops—which is what I had told Edna, but I think we both know that's not going to be the case. The house is full, top to bottom, with odds and ends that Vera collected over the years. There are so many bedrooms and bathrooms and sitting rooms and rooms I have yet to explore. It's going to take me weeks, if not months or years, to go through everything and make a decision on what to keep. Some of it is really valuable, while other things might hold sentimental value.

If there's anything left of my mom's, I want to be sure I find it, which means I need to take my time. Every decision left to do with Bitter House is mine.

Though that isn't new information, I feel more alone than I ever have as I stare around the empty room processing it for what seems like the first time. The emptiness of the house, the silence of it, weighs on me.

I'm digging through the drawers of the desk, trying to decide what should be kept and what can be discarded when I hear the front door open.

My heart stalls.

I should've locked the door, but the gate keeps everyone out, so it didn't cross my mind.

"Edna?" I call, standing up as I move toward the empty doorway of the room I'm currently in, studying it for signs of the intruder.

My mouse-quiet and cautious footsteps slow even more as the person comes into view. My breathing catches in my chest, a ball of oxygen refusing to move another inch until I wake up from this dream.

Nightmare.

Because that's what it is. What it has to be. There is simply no other explanation.

"Bridget." A word, not a question. He doesn't look surprised to see me at all.

I swallow, dusting a hand over my stomach as fury heats under every inch of my skin, like a marshmallow smoldering over a fire. "What the hell are you doing here, Cole?"

He looks just like he did before. Darkness incarnate. Dark hair that is entirely too full and perfect. Dark eyes, and if I was close enough, I'd be able to see the flecks of amber that decorate them, like they're waiting to catch dragonflies and hold them forever. Waiting to catch anything that will fall into their trap.

Thankfully, I was never so foolish.

The beard is new, I realize, as he runs a hand over it. His brows lift as he smirks at me, then looks away with a scoff. "She didn't tell you."

Again, not a question.

"What do you mean? Tell me what?"

I don't like being on the end of a conversation that holds no answers. Desperately don't like it when Cole knows more than I do.

He shoves his hands into his pockets. "Vera left me Bitter House."

"No, she didn't." The response is instant. Knee-jerk. It's impossible. He's lying. Why is he here? What does he want? "Are you crazy? Call your mom. She's the executor. The house is mine."

He holds up a finger, looking so freaking arrogant I want to smack him. "Actually, it's *ours*. She left it to both of us." His lips quirk with the threat of a smile. "*You* call my mom and ask. I'll wait."

"You're lying." He has to be lying. This doesn't make any sense. I was never supposed to have to see him again.

"Oh, come on. You know me better than that." He gives me a cocky grin and turns, walking down the hall and away from me without another word.

This already terrible day has just been amplified by a thousand, and he couldn't care less. He doesn't want this house, doesn't care about Bitter House except maybe to extract money from its sale. But clearly he's taking pleasure out of driving me mad.

I won't let it happen. There has to be a simple explanation. A way to fix this.

Grabbing my phone, I search for Edna's name in my recent call log and select it. Within seconds, she answers, as if she's been expecting to hear from me.

"Bridget," she says with a cheery voice. "Hello, honey. Did you make it there alright?"

"Why is Cole here?" I ask, avoiding the niceties.

She lets out a slow sigh. "I...Bridget, I didn't know. I had no idea Vera had left him half of Bitter House until I saw the will. I was just as shocked as you are."

"It's impossible," I sputter. "You're serious. She...she left it for both of us. Why? Half the house? How is any of that supposed to work? I don't understand. *Why?* Why would she do this? She knows we don't get along. Could she really have wanted to be this cruel?" It's a stupid question, one that doesn't require an answer. Vera was cruel through and through. I shouldn't be surprised that her final act was to further twist the knife.

I hear a soft exhale of breath, like she's trying to decide how to respond. Eventually, her answer comes. "I don't think she was doing any of this to be cruel, sweetheart. Truly, I don't. This was... I wish I had an explanation. I wish she had told me something, given me a heads-up, so that I could help you both through this, but I have to believe this was her way of making things right. Of trying to help you both."

Vera has never helped anyone but herself, but pointing that out will only make things worse right now. "What are we supposed to do?" I ask her. "What are we supposed to do with the house, Edna? How is this supposed to work? Can't you just talk to him? Tell him this isn't right? We all know we can't stay here together, and if he won't agree to sell it, what happens?"

"Well..." She pauses, thinking. "If you don't want the house, if you have no plans to stay there, perhaps you would consider giving it to him. Letting him buy you out of your half."

My vision blurs with anger. Even though, just minutes ago, I was sure I didn't want to stay here, the idea of giving it to Cole is unthinkable. I would sooner burn it to the ground. "Absolutely not. How can you ask me to do that? Why didn't you tell me about this before I arrived? Warn me that this was happening? That he would be here."

Her voice goes soft and breathy. "We both know why I didn't. I'm sorry, but if I had told you Cole would be there, you wouldn't have shown up, and I needed you to help me handle things. Both of you."

"So you lied to me? You set me up?" Tears well in my eyes over yet another betrayal. That seems to be all this house brings me.

"I wasn't trying to lie. I'm sorry. I'm so, so sorry. I can only do what the will asks of me, and I'm trying to navigate uncharted waters myself. Vera had it stated very clearly that you and Cole were to be given equal shares of the property. I'm sorry, honey. I know this is a difficult time, and I never meant to make it worse for you—"

"Difficult time," I scoff.

"Bridget, please—"

"I have to go."

She doesn't argue. We both know there's no point. What's done is done, and now, once again, I'm left to pick up the pieces of my grandmother's decision.

CHAPTER TWO

BRIDGET

"What did you do?" After I get off the phone with Edna, I track Cole to the kitchen, launching myself at him as if I were a predator and he is my prey. "Did you blackmail her? There is absolutely no way my grandmother would've left you the house. It's not yours."

He stands on the opposite side of the island with the most casual expression on his face I've ever seen, like we're discussing dinner options and not our futures.

"Legally, I'm afraid, it is. It's both of ours."

"No."

He turns away from me, opening the double doors of the fridge and sifting through what's inside. "Look," he calls over his shoulder, "like it or not, the house was left to both of us. So now we have to decide how to move forward."

"I will sue you. I'll take you to court and sue you. I'll say you manipulated her. That you took advantage of her."

Clearly unfazed, he retrieves a tray of fruit from somewhere inside the fridge, sniffs it, and places it on the island, popping a grape into his mouth. "Go ahead. Be my guest. You can try to fight it all you want, but you won't be able to prove anything because there's nothing to prove. I didn't manipulate Vera. Hell, I was just as surprised as you clearly are. But come on, B. Pick your jaw up off the floor, and let's move on."

I snap my jaw shut on command, glaring at him. "Why would she leave the house to both of us?"

He shrugs one shoulder. "Great question. One that I would like an answer to as well, in fact. What did my mom tell you?"

"She said Vera didn't tell her anything either. She had no idea, aside from knowing that she was the executor, until she read over the will with her lawyer."

"Vera hadn't lost her mind," he says. "She was coherent when she died. Stubborn as ever. Whatever choice she made, it was hers. She had a reason."

Something flutters in my chest. "You were with her?"

"Not on the day...no. But leading up to it, I was here with Mom. She didn't leave her side." He looks down as he says it, as if he's apologizing, though what I'm not sure. He knows Vera and I had a strained relationship more than most people, since he had a front-row seat for most of it. In fairness, his view of our relationship is one of the only ones that exists, since Vera and I were never seen in public together. She couldn't be bothered to do anything for me. Edna was always responsible for whatever I needed.

I cross my arms. "Okay, well, what are we going to do about this situation? It's ridiculous."

"What would you *like* to do about it?"

"I'd *like* you to do the right thing and give me my house."

"*Our* house."

He's infuriating. I groan, squeezing my hands into fists at either side of my head. "I'm not planning to sell it," I say firmly, stomping my foot as if I'm stamping the statement onto the tile beneath my feet, making it true. If selling Bitter House means handing it over to Cole, I'll stay until the walls crumble all around me.

"Glad we're on the same page about that."

I blink, tilting my head to the side. "Really? You weren't hoping to sell it and flit off into the sunset somewhere, instantly rich?"

He leans across the counter, staring at me. "Okay, one, I don't *flit* anywhere. I'm not a finch. And two, did it ever occur to you that I actually enjoyed my time here? That I might want to keep this house and couldn't care less about the money?"

"No." The answer comes in an instant. "In the ten seconds I've had to process this, I guess I didn't consider that you'd lost your mind and might actually want to stay here. It's impossible."

His dark brows draw down. "Why?"

I try to force the million reasons out of my mouth all at once and end up stammering over my words. "Because... because we hate each other. We can't stay here, and there's no way in hell I'm leaving you with the house. I could..." I try to think, pacing the tile floor. "I could buy you out."

I couldn't. I can't. I'm flat broke, working an entry-level office job and splitting a two-bedroom apartment with my best friend and her two cats. I'd have to check my account balance before I bought a coffee at this point, let alone a house.

I'm equal parts relieved and dismayed to hear his answer.

"Not interested."

It's as if I'm a sheet of cracking glass—each sentence from him, each stupid smirk, a hint more pressure from his palm, another splinter. "Cole, please... Let's just be civil about this. It's my house, not yours. You have to know that. How can we fix this? You know you don't want this place. Not really. It's a lot of work."

"I don't mind work."

I flatten my palms on the countertop. "It belongs to my family."

"It belongs to the two of us now, not your family. In fact, Mom said Vera only left Jenn, Zach, and Jonah money. No property. I'm sure they were thrilled to hear that."

"They weren't close. She stopped talking to any of them years ago. I was all she had." My voice cracks at the truth of that statement. I was all she had, and I was never enough.

He looks like he wants to say something, to argue and further push me toward breaking, but instead, he turns his attention back to the food in front of him, meticulously picking out a strawberry, studying it, then taking a bite.

"We can't do this. Please. Please be reasonable. I just lost her. Don't put me through this."

"I'm not doing anything, B. I'm really not trying to be difficult or cruel, but Vera left me the house, too. I was the one who stayed here after you left. Maybe that meant something to her—"

"After I *left*?!" I shout, casting my arms out to my sides. "As if I had a choice. I was kicked out."

His tone remains calm and cool. "Regardless, I was here. I've been here. I stayed."

A shard of ice slides down my throat. "You stayed? In this house? With Vera?"

"My mom was here until the end. I visited, yes. I was here when you weren't. And I don't know what sort of beef you two had, I don't know what happened, but what I do know is that I loved this house. I spent just as much time here as you did, and if Vera wanted to leave it to me, I'm not going to question it. I have no interest in selling and, from what I understand, we can't do that until everything with the will is settled anyway. Probate, or whatever. So we're stuck together." He rounds the island slowly, eyes on me. "I can't afford to buy your half from you outright, and I don't want to, but if you don't want the house anymore—if you want to work out some sort of payment arrangement for me to buy it from you, we can talk about that, too. Or..."

"Or?" I stare at him.

"Or we could make this work. It could be a vacation home or...we could be roommates. Something. At least until we decide how we want to move forward."

I cross my arms. "I'm not going anywhere. You'd change the locks."

One corner of his mouth quirks, and he makes no effort to deny it. "Then I guess we're stuck with each other for the foreseeable future."

"I guess we are." This is the worst day of my life.

"I'll be in my old room then, roomie." He walks past me —saunters, practically—and I listen as he jogs up the steps.

What the hell were you thinking, Vera? There's no way this ends without one of us being murdered and the other in jail. Maybe that's what she was hoping for. One final kick to the gut courtesy of the woman who was supposed to love me.

His door shuts upstairs, and I squeeze my eyes shut. A knock on the front door interrupts my internal panic, and when I cross the room, hurry down the hall, and open it, I find a woman with a familiar face, though I can't quite place her.

"Oh. Hi." Her gray hair is pulled back in a bun, and she's wearing a floral blouse and jeans, looking perfectly put together despite the tears in her bright blue eyes. Her chin quivers. "Bridget, right?"

I grip the door tighter as I notice two other women walking up behind her, one dressed in a calf-length dress and the other in yoga pants and a T-shirt. They're all around Vera's age, though a bit younger—sixties or seventies if I had to guess. One dusts her silver hair back from her eyes, while the other uses the bouquet of flowers in her hand to shield herself from the misting rain that has set in.

"Do I know you?" I ask the woman at the door, taking half a step back.

"Not really, no. I haven't seen you since you were very young," she says, waving a hand as if to shoo away my worry. She points behind her. "I'm Jane. This is Lily." The dress and a head full of long, silver waves. "And Cate." Yoga pants with a graying-blonde bob. "We're the neighbors. We were friends of your grandmother. Of Vera." Her voice cracks at the sound of my grandmother's name, and she puts a hand to her chest. "We're so very sorry for your loss."

"Oh." She looks as if she wants me to open the door, but I don't. I'm not about to be swindled by these women. Vera didn't have friends aside from Edna, whom she paid to stick around. She was perpetually alone, but I don't say any of these things. Instead, I give a small, sad smile and say, "Thank you."

"Well, anyway, I know you probably don't want three old ladies interrupting you when you've just gotten here and are dealing with so much. We just wanted to stop by and see if there's anything we can do to help you get settled in. Truly, put us to work if we can help with anything you need. Grocery runs, cleaning, sorting through Vera's things. She was very special to us. It's the least we can do. Oh, and we brought some flowers and a few meals."

It's the first time I notice the rectangular cloth bag sitting at her feet, and she bends and lifts it up. "There are two pans in here, one is lasagna and the other is chicken enchiladas. You can pop one right in the oven to warm it up and save the other in the freezer. I wasn't sure what you liked, but we wanted to do something."

The women join her on the porch now, handing me the flowers and the bag containing the meals. It's heavier than I expected, and when I peer inside, there are two glass Pyrex baking dishes, one stacked on top of the other.

"Do you want us to help get everything inside?" the dress-wearing woman, Lily, asks.

"Um—"

I feel rather than hear or see him as he approaches me from behind. There's a shift in the air, and the three women's eyes lift from mine to something behind me.

Jane's face splits into a smile. "Cole. Well, there you are!"

He slips past me, giving each of the women a familiar hug. "Jane, looking beautiful as ever." He hugs Cate and Lily next, peppering them with similar compliments.

"You old charmer." Cate swats his shoulder, though Lily looks unimpressed and only hugs him with one limp arm.

"We just brought over flowers and some meals for you two," Jane tells him, gesturing toward the items I'm now holding. Her eyes crinkle with concern. "How are you holding up?"

To my surprise, it's Cole she's looking at, not me. They also don't seem to be the least bit shocked to have found us both here. It's almost like they knew we'd be here, that Vera told them her evil plan.

Cole holds out his hands, prepared to take the food from me, but I turn away, so he shoves his hands into his pockets instead without missing a beat. "We're taking it day by day," he says eventually. "It was really nice of you ladies to drop this off. I'll help Bridget get it all inside now, if you don't mind. But we'll see you soon, I'm sure."

"Of course. We're always around," Cate says.

"If you need anything, you just let us know." That's Jane. "Don't be strangers."

"Soak those dishes," Lily calls.

Cole nods and waves, ushering me back into the house. When the door shuts, I dart to a window, waiting and watching to make sure they're leaving. When I see the three women depart, I turn back to find a smug-looking Cole staring at me. "Can I help with something?" He holds out his hands.

"No." I huff. "Who are they? Why do they know you so well?"

"They're neighbors. Friends of Vera's."

"Vera didn't have any friends."

He sighs. "Look, it doesn't matter, okay? They were just trying to be nice. Do you want me to help you put everything away or not?"

"No. I've got it." I storm past him and into the kitchen, placing one tray of food in the fridge and the other in the freezer.

Why do I once again feel like an outsider in my own home?

CHAPTER THREE

BRIDGET

I hardly slept, even with a belly full of the lasagna Jane dropped off.

I'm not an idiot, of course. I waited until Cole had eaten a whole piece before I tried it, just in case. But once I was sure it was safe, I had to give in to my hunger and eat it.

I don't know why I'm so bothered by the neighbors. I'm sure Cole's right—they were just trying to do something nice—but I don't like the fact that they all seem to be aware of something I'm not. That they're making me feel unwelcome or not part of this. Like they all know more than me about this situation. And I guess they do.

For the past twelve years, I have no idea what has gone on in Vera's life. I don't know who she was when she died, but they do. The fact that they know more than me burns like sandpaper against skin.

I make my way downstairs and to the kitchen, where I pour myself a glass of sparkling water with lemon, thankful the house is still quiet. If the Cole upstairs is anything like the Cole I once knew, he'll be asleep until somewhere around three this afternoon. What does he even do with his life anymore?

After dinner, he disappeared, and I haven't heard from him since. Does he work? Shouldn't he be leaving to go somewhere? I could ask Edna, I suppose, but I've always made it a point not to mention her son unless I have no other choice, to prevent her from considering it an olive branch when she knows we've always hated each other. Besides that, I'm still mad at her for not preparing me for this.

I cross the kitchen and make my way down the hall and toward the door, planning to check and see if his car is still in the driveway. If he made the mistake of leaving, I'm changing the locks. I'll let the lawyers do what they will—I'll say I was concerned for my safety if I have to, but there's no way he's getting back into this house if he so much as takes a single step outside of it.

In the driveway, his black SUV still sits next to my Camry. I suck in a disappointed breath. I knew it wouldn't be that easy, but that doesn't mean I didn't have hope.

I'm nothing if not foolishly stubborn and occasionally optimistic.

As I step back to shut the door, something resting on the mat catches my eyes.

I look down to find a brown envelope with a red ribbon tied around it, dropped just over the letters E and L in 'Welcome.'

I look up and around, searching for the person who must've delivered this letter directly to my doorstep, then cautiously bend down and pick it up.

It's heavier than I expected, the envelope made from a thick, textured paper that feels old, though I suspect it's not since there's no visible wear on it. No one has labeled it—there's no name or even address—which means someone brought it here and left it for me to find.

Or...*someone* to find, anyway.

Perhaps Cole is the intended recipient.

I glance behind me in the house, worried he's woken up and is somewhere watching me, but with the reassurance he's not, I check over my shoulder to the driveway once more and then step inside the house.

In the kitchen, I untie the ribbon and use my fingernail to pry the envelope open carefully. Inside, there's a folded paper the same khaki color as the envelope. I pull it out slowly and unfold it, dropping the envelope on the island. The letter is typed, further confirming it's not nearly as old as it looks.

It's also addressed to me.

Bridget,

Vera was not who you thought she was. There are things you should know, things I wish I didn't have to tell you. But someone must, so you can do what is right.

Vera Bitter had secrets. Secrets so dangerous they nearly ruined her life. She was careless with them, chose them over her family. Over you.

I want to tell you everything, Bridget, and I know you have no reason to trust me, but I hope in time you will. I will write six additional letters. Each of those letters will contain a secret.

By the end, I hope you will make the right choice. Please don't do anything or make any decisions until you've received each of the six remaining letters. You'll want to hear all I have to say.

Signed,
A friend

P.S. Keep your doors locked.

I read through the letter twice, turning it over in case there's some hint on the back that I may have missed about who sent it, but there's nothing. It feels like a sick joke.

I knew Vera as well as anyone did, though I'm not delusional enough to think anyone truly knew her. She preferred it that way. I read the last line again: *Keep your doors locked.*

What is that supposed to mean?

Is it a threat?

Fear grips me somewhere deep in my belly, quickly replaced by anger. How dare they! If someone is trying to scare me, there's only one person I can think of who could benefit from that.

I storm out of the kitchen and up the stairs, taking two at a time, and rap my knuckles on the wood of his door. I'm furious by the time he pulls it open, one eye closed, torso shirtless, hair a mess.

"Yeah?"

"It won't work."

"Good morning to you, too," he grumbles.

I slam the letter into his chest. "Whatever your plan is, whatever you hoped would happen when I read this, you're wrong. If you're trying to scare me away from here, it won't work. I'm not going to be run off by your little games. I'm not going anywhere, no matter what you do. So you might as well just give up now. You won't win."

"Win?" he asks under his breath, turning the letter over and reading it slowly, rubbing a fist over his eye to brush away the sleep. "I..." When he looks up, his expression is unreadable, jaw slack. "You think I wrote this?" He flips it over, checking the back. "Where did you even get this?"

"Don't play dumb. I know you left it on the porch for me to find."

He looks down at the paper again, shaking his head. "I have no idea what you're talking about. I didn't write this. I've never seen it before."

The defiance in his voice almost makes me believe him—*almost*.

"Stop it. I know—"

He laughs. "Stop what? I'm serious, B. It wasn't me."

"Don't call me B."

"Everyone calls you B." He holds the letter out toward me, and I snatch it back.

"My friends call me B, and you are not a friend."

"Fine." His lips form a hard line. "I didn't write the letter. Believe what you want."

"Who else could've? The gate is locked. It was on the porch, not in the mailbox. No one else had access."

His jaw drops open as if I'm being ridiculous. "No one else had access? Are you serious? So many people had access! Jane, Cate, and Lily were *literally* just here. Mom has the code, too. And the gardener. The maintenance man. The mail woman. Who knows who all Vera gave the code to. It's not just me."

I pause. He's not wrong. Over the years, countless people have been given the gate code, which hasn't changed for as long as I can remember. Still...the mail woman has no reason to want me to be afraid of this house. Cole does.

"Well, what do you think it means?" I ask, studying the letter again.

"Sounds like she had secrets, and someone plans to expose them," he says plainly, clearly not concerned. His voice goes dry and sarcastic as he says, "Someone who obviously doesn't understand how blackmail works."

"It's someone trying to scare me."

He twists his lips in thought, reaching across the bed and grabbing a shirt to throw on. "I think that's a bit dramatic."

"Keep your doors locked?"

"A good reminder, don't you think?" He nods, walking past me and into his bathroom, leaving the door open.

I stay put, confused about what is happening until I hear his electric toothbrush running. "What secrets could Vera have possibly had?"

It takes him a moment to answer as he spits and pauses the toothbrush. "Probably sex stuff."

I scowl. "Stop."

He laughs, turning the toothbrush back on, and I storm from the room. As per usual, he's absolutely no help.

CHAPTER FOUR

BRIDGET

When I was little, I was obsessed with water. Pools, bathtubs, the pond behind Bitter House. You name it, and I was in it every chance I got. Though so much of my life has changed since then, that's one thing that hasn't changed at all.

As I slip into the pool in the backyard, my body seems to relax in an instant. Despite everything going on, this is the one place—submerged in water—where I can shut everything else off, quiet my mind, and just exist. Where, for at least a few minutes, I'm a mermaid on an adventure and not a woman in way over her head.

I lean into that, swimming and flipping and floating, holding my breath and diving and spinning like a kid. Forgetting everything and everyone. I even forget about the letter, at least for a short while.

I dive under the water, skimming my stomach against the concrete floor of the deep end just because I can, then flip over and stare up at the sun's reflection against the rippling water.

When my lungs burn for oxygen, I relent, pushing up toward the surface with all my might. As I burst out of the water, I gasp for air, flicking my hair back over my head.

A voice in the distance stops me.

"And the garden, clearly. What about the backyard?"

It's a man's voice. One I don't recognize.

"It's gated."

"And the pool? Is it this way?"

I slip out of the water, the noise drowning out whatever response may have been given, and march toward their voices, dripping wet and too furious to care.

As I round the corner of the house, walking out of the pool gate, I spot Cole—barefoot and dressed in a T-shirt and jeans—and a man in a suit and tie. The man has that look about him, like realtors and car salesmen. A giant, fake smile, charm oozing from his every pore. He eyes me with admiration that feels completely fake.

"What the hell is going on?" I shout at them both.

The man chuckles, glancing at Cole as if to say *women, right?* "You must be the lady of the house. I'm with Pearson and Pearson Real Estate."

I glance at his hand with disgust. "And?"

He recovers, tucking it back into his pocket. "*And* I received a call this morning that you might want to list this property."

Rage explodes in me like a ball of fire, washing over every inch of my skin from the inside. "Oh you did?" My lips form a hard line as I pin Cole with a stare. "Who would that call have been from?"

"Not me," Cole says, hands up in the air. "I already told him we aren't selling."

"The call was from a woman." The man reaches into his jacket pocket, pulling out his phone. "I don't mean to cause any trouble. I...I spoke to a Bridget Lancaster." He looks up. "Do you know her?"

It's as if the ground has opened up under my feet. "That's impossible. *I'm* Bridget Lancaster. I didn't call you."

I can tell he doesn't believe me. His gaze travels to the house as if he can't help it. "Well, what do you say we take a look around and see where it leads? You can always say no, but what would it hurt to hear my thoughts on the property and its value? If you disagree with my numbers, I'll walk away with no hard feelings, but I can tell you right now, you won't disagree." He glances up at the house again. "I'm positive you're going to like what numbers I come up with." He holds out his hand again. "What do you say? I'm the best there is, and I can make sure you're set for life with this sale, guaranteed."

Cole's eyes flick to me with something that looks vaguely like amusement, the way my roommate, Ana, always watches her cats whenever Teddy—the younger, cocky boy—pounces toward Olivia—the older, grouchy girl—and we just wait for her to put him in his place.

"The house isn't for sale," I say flatly. "And I'd appreciate it if you'd get off our property."

He opens his mouth, clearly already prepared to

respond, but hesitates. I've thrown him off guard. "Are you...
are you sure? Like I said—"

"I'm positive."

He looks at Cole, clearly hoping he'll come to his
defense, but Cole's eyebrows merely rise. "I told you."

The man takes a step back. "Can I leave you with my
number in case you change your mind?"

"We won't." I hold up my hand to stop him as he
reaches for his pocket. "Thanks for coming, and goodbye."

With that, the man retreats. When he's gone, I turn to
find Cole smirking.

"What's so funny?"

It takes him a while to answer. "You said *our* property."

"I'm nothing if not accurate." I sigh. "How did he get
the gate code?"

"I buzzed him inside, but I didn't know who he was."

"Are you serious? Don't let anyone in. Are you crazy?
The letter said to keep the doors locked."

"He seemed harmless, and he was asking for you. He said
you called him. I would *never* stand in the way of you and
your guests." His tone is light and teasing, feigning
formality.

"I won't be having any *guests*." I mirror his words and
tone back to him.

His eyes flick down over me, and if I didn't know better,
I would swear he was checking me out.

"Noted." He turns away, heading back for the house.

"Where are you going?"

"Back to *our* house. Enjoy your swim."

CHAPTER FIVE

BRIDGET

I spend another hour outside by the pool before returning to the house. Though I'd tucked my key safely in my shoe, just in case Cole decided to lock me out, I found the door unlocked and my housemate-slash-archenemy in the kitchen, humming to himself while he sifted through the fridge.

Upstairs, I towel dry my hair and change into dry clothes, vaguely considering putting on makeup but landing on just a bit of ChapStick for my lips and some lotion for my skin instead.

Downstairs, Cole is still in the kitchen, but I'm surprised to find him leaning over a pot on the stove. The air is filled with a hint of something warm and savory.

"What are you doing?"

He glances over his shoulder, like he's been expecting me. "What's it look like?"

"Preparing whatever you plan to poison me with."

He draws his lips together, clearly unamused. "That's one way to say, 'Thanks for cooking dinner, Cole. You're the best.'"

"Since when do you cook?" This feels like a trap, though I don't actually think he'd poison me. Putting something in our meal to make me sick, though? That I could see.

Instead of the snarky response I'm expecting, he shrugs and turns back to the pot. "I like cooking, actually. I don't like fast foods, so I had to learn."

"What are you making?"

"You don't recognize the smell?"

I inhale deeply and shake my head. "I don't think so. Should I?"

"Mom's stuffed pepper soup."

Something in my chest softens as he says the words. When I was growing up and had a hard day, it was one of Edna's go-to recipes. A pang of sadness I wasn't expecting hits me out of nowhere. Growing up under the cold shadow of Vera, Edna was all but a second mother to me. She was the one who explained periods to me. She helped me dress for prom and took me to get my hair cut whenever I needed it. Though she was Vera's house manager, we all knew she was more than that. She took care of everything, me included, until she didn't.

Aside from occasional text messages or phone calls to check in or wish me a happy birthday, I haven't heard from her since Vera had her pack my things, put them in a car, and send me on my way.

I still don't understand how anyone could do that to

someone they were supposed to care about. Vera's betrayal was painful enough, but the pain of Edna siding with her cut deeper.

Cole has turned away from me, returning his attention to the food, so I cross the room and open the refrigerator. I grab a bottle of sparkling water, clicking my tongue.

"Does your mom still shop for the house?" I can't help my curiosity over when I'll see her again, even though I'm not sure I want to.

"Officially, not since Vera died, but she stocked the house before we got here."

"We're going to have to figure that out, then."

"Shopping?" At that, he turns his full body toward me, clearly amused.

"Yeah. We're going to run out of things eventually. We'll have to shop for things. We need to find out how to take over paying the bills, and I mean, I guess we'll be splitting everything. I have no idea how much it costs to heat and cool a place like this. Plus, there are repairs to think about." Stress zips through me like lightning, and I feel a headache forming in my temples. I'm in way over my head here, but I can't admit it. I refuse to.

"We'll split everything down the middle, and we can shop for ourselves, like normal roommates." He teases me with a sly grin. "Though we only have to label things if you really, really want to."

"Oh, I'll be triple labeling my things."

The smile disappears, and he gives me a dramatic sigh. "Suit yourself."

I twist the top off my bottle and move to stand next to the stove, watching him. "So, your mom really told you I'd be here, that this would be the arrangement, before you got here? And you still came? You thought this was a good idea?"

He stirs the soup thoughtfully. "Define *good*."

I roll my eyes.

"I thought it was necessary," he says after a moment. "It was what Vera wanted."

"God knows we can't have things going against her wishes."

"She did what she thought was best."

"Oh, always."

Resting the spoon on the stovetop, he studies me, a wrinkle forming between his eyes. "Look, I don't know what happened back then."

I wait for him to say more.

"I woke up one morning, and you were just...gone."

Despite his many flaws, I've never known Cole to be dishonest, so I'm inclined to trust him, but it doesn't make it easier to swallow the truth. "I'm sure it made your life better."

His dark brows draw together. "Who says you ever affected my life one way or the other?"

He's right. I'm assuming he cared at all, when we both know he didn't. Somehow, that stings worse. I sink against the counter. "Whatever. It doesn't matter anymore. What are we going to do about the house?"

He crosses the room and pulls a beer from the fridge. "Wait for all the secrets to be revealed, obviously."

"Cole."

His head spins toward me, eyes locking on mine with something like shock in his expression. He swallows, looking away. "There's nothing we can do yet. We have to wait for everything to get settled with the estate and—"

A knock on the door interrupts whatever he was planning to say.

"Are you expecting anyone?" I ask.

He shakes his head, moving past me and down the hall. "It might be my mom."

The idea of seeing Edna again fills me with conflicting emotions—a mixture of hope and fear. I don't want to have to rehash all that happened again, and yet all I want is for her to hug me and promise it's all going to work out. Sometimes, I hate the part of myself that is still very much that little girl who needed her. I hate that I ever needed anyone, when all they've ever done is hurt me, betray me, or let me down.

But when Cole opens the door, all my worry has been for nothing. It's not Edna there waiting for us, but a tall, blonde woman with a round stomach and wide hips. Her breasts have been shoved into a blouse that looks two sizes too small. She pins me with a glare, and I recognize her instantly. Vera had the same glare.

"Aunt Jenn."

Her eyes widen slightly. "So it's true." She looks past me

and into the hallway, stepping inside without warning. "She left you the house."

It doesn't really seem like a question, but I look at Cole. "Well, actually, she left it to both of us."

She drops her jaw, staring between us. "The *two* of you? Who are you? The son of the help?" She sneers, looking back at me. "What did you say to her? Why did she do this?"

At my side, Cole is surprisingly quiet.

"I don't know. Neither of us do. We found out after she died," I say.

She blows an indignant breath through her nose. "Well, clearly it's a mistake."

"Edna said she left you an inheritance."

Her eyes flame with rage. "Edna should keep her nose where it belongs. Wait a minute." She lifts her chin and sniffs —she literally sniffs the air, as if she might be able to track her down like a bloodhound. "Is she here?"

"Who? Edna?"

"No. She's not here. My mom moved out after Vera's death. She's staying in my apartment until she finds a place of her own." Cole's voice drips with venom. "She's doing exactly what Vera wanted her to, just like she always has. And, for the record, the will is literally, legally, *her* business."

Jenn wrinkles her nose, her wrist bent up near her shoulder like she's afraid to touch anything—as if being poor is contagious—as she turns her attention back to me. "Well, clearly, it's a mistake. She wouldn't have left the house to you. No offense. I'm her daughter."

Cole steps next to me, his shoulder brushing mine. It

sends a wave of electricity down my body that I'm not prepared for. "Bridget's mom was her daughter, too. She left Bridget the house for a reason." Something about him standing up for me has my muscles smoothing out like I've slipped into a warm bath. The feeling is foreign.

"Be that as it may, I'm going to fight it," she says. "No judge in his right mind would let this stand."

A bitter, acrid taste settles in the back of my throat. "Be our guest."

She shakes her head, looking around the room with haunted eyes. I wonder if she can still smell Vera here, the way I can. "This was never the plan. My mother could be cold, but this...this is beyond what she was capable of. She was going to leave the house to me. Her only living daughter. You're stealing it from me. You, Bridget Lancaster, are a thief. In this house or not, you'll never be a Bitter."

"I—"

"*How dare you?* You have no idea what you're talking about. Bridget may as well have been a daughter to her." Cole's tone is sour, angry as he steps in front of me. "You have no right to claim you know what Vera wanted, or to make Bridget feel bad for something she had no say in."

Jenn's chilling blue eyes lock on Cole as a block of ice slides down my ribcage. "Yes, you certainly would come to her defense, wouldn't you? This is all just too convenient for you, isn't it? How do we know this wasn't some weird trick by you and that twisted mother of yours? I always told my sister I thought Edna was after Vera's money, and now she's gone and proven me right, just used you as her pawn. I'll bet you two are laughing all the way to the bank, aren't you? Bridget is just too naïve to see it. If your mother were here, Bridget, she'd agree with me. She always did."

I don't think that's true. I only ever heard my mother and father speak kindly of Edna from what I remember, though it isn't much. Still, I don't respond, searching my memory for anything that might hint that Jenn is right. After all, Edna betrayed me once. Could she be doing the same now?

Cole is quiet for a second, the room eerily still. When he speaks, his voice is softer, lower. Somehow, it's even more threatening. Like the first vibrations of an earthquake. "My mother was the closest thing Vera ever had to a friend. She cared about her, even when Vera did nothing to deserve it. And, as you well know, she was left nothing in her will. The house was left to me and Bridget, but all the money went to you. And your children. My mother isn't getting a dime."

She sneers. "I'll bet she hates that."

"Edna deserved a lot more than Vera left her," I say firmly. "After all she did for her, and for this family. But the money never mattered to her." I cross my arms. "I don't know why you're so upset about the house. It's not like you grew up here. *We* did." I move my thumb back and forth between Cole and me. "It's ours, and Vera knew that."

Cole steps backward, his eyes on mine as our shoulders brush once again. It's clear he didn't expect me to stand up for him, but right now it feels like it's us against the world. Two little outcasts ruling the castle. "It's ours," he agrees. "Feel free to fight that, but until you're able to, unless someone tells us you've won, we're going to have to ask you to leave and not come back."

She scoffs. "You can't kick me out of my family house." As if to prove her point, she stalks across the room and takes a seat at the desk. "I'm not leaving, and I'm certainly not listening to a child."

Next to me, Cole bristles, but before he can argue or make this worse, I switch tactics.

"Please don't do this," I say softly. "I don't want it to be like this between us. We're family. You're...you're the only family I still have. Even if we haven't stayed in touch over the years, I know my mom would want us to fix this. You were her sister. She loved you." My voice cracks as I say it, knowing how true it is.

Her face softens slightly, somewhere around the eyes. I never really knew my aunt, and I knew my cousins even less. When I was a kid, my family was close. We visited Bitter House for birthday parties and Christmases, family dinners, and Thanksgivings, but those days are just distant memories. We haven't spoken in years, but with Vera gone, they're the only thing I have. They're my only remaining connection to my mother. To my past.

"I don't know what happened between Vera and the rest of the family. When I was younger, you guys were around more, and then...you just stopped coming."

"That was never my decision," Jenn says, refusing to look at me. "My mother always had things her way. You know how she was."

"Well, it's not how I want it. As long as I'm here, if we

can be civil, I'd love for it to go back to the family I remember from before Mom died. The holidays and the get-togethers, don't you miss those days? Because I do. I know it can't be fixed overnight, but I'd love to find a place to start. Maybe we could get together for dinner or something. I just...I want to get to know you. All of you. I haven't seen Jonah or Zach since we were all kids. It shouldn't be like that. We don't have to be the family Vera left. We can do it our own way."

She twists her lips with a response I can't quite read, so I press on.

"I never meant for any of this to hurt you. Believe me, I was just as shocked as you are about the house, but I have to trust that there was a reason Vera left it to me. To us," I correct myself before Cole gets the chance. "It may belong to me, but you're welcome to visit any time. I'd love it if you did."

She sighs. "You just don't get it, Bridget. The money is one thing, but the house is...it's what she worked for. Fought to keep after our father died when my uncle wanted it, when the original Bitter family tried to take it back. It was mine. Maybe not for the first few years of my life, until my grandparents died when I was a teenager, but it was my home nonetheless."

"Regardless"—Cole steps in again—"the house belongs to both of us. If you'd like to make us an offer to buy it, we can't stop you. But we won't just be giving it to you, and it will take both of us to agree to sell it, which we haven't done. We aren't taking any part of this decision lightly. We want to respect Vera's final wishes." With that, he turns and holds out an arm. "Now, if you'll excuse us, we were just getting ready to have dinner, and you're interrupting."

Aunt Jenn bristles, her shoulders going stiff as she stands. Her eyes dart to me, and I shake my head. "He's right. I know emotions are running high right now, and we all just need some time to cool off. Maybe we could make plans for you to visit on another day."

She huffs. "We'll see about that." With that, she marches from the room, shoving Cole's arm away when he attempts to pull the door open for her.

When the door shuts, I turn back to him, but he's already returning to the kitchen to stir the soup.

"Did Vera really not leave anything for Edna in the will?" I ask, following close behind him.

He glances over his shoulder. "She didn't leave her any money."

"But she left her something?"

His head bobs up and down. "Some jewelry, I think. Her old clothing. Mom didn't want any of it, so it's all still here at the house for us to sort through. That wasn't why she was here." The defensive tone of his voice catches me by surprise.

"Okay. I'm not saying it was. I was just asking a question."

"I don't like the fact that Jenn thinks Mom was using Vera. If anything, it was the other way around. You saw how much she did for this place. For all of us."

I fold my arms across my chest. "I know that, but Jenn doesn't. She wasn't here for most of it, not once Vera sent her away. I think it's normal for her to be...concerned. You didn't have to be so mean to her."

"Oh, I didn't? You mean after she insulted the both of us and my mom? What exactly should I have done, Bridget? Offered for her to join us for dinner? Clearly that was your plan."

"She's family. And she's upset. Understandably so. It's a tense time for all of us."

He rolls his eyes, jaw set. "She hadn't spoken to Vera since you were, what? Ten years old? The fact that she got an inheritance at all was more than generous—"

"She's her daughter. Of course she got an inheritance. And she's right. Staying away wasn't her choice. Vera sent everyone away, just like she did me. It wasn't always like that before. If I was old enough when she cut ties with everyone else, I would've been sent away at the same time."

"I'm sure she had her reasons, and I'd bet they had something to do with money. You were just a kid. You couldn't have seen or understood everything."

Something about the way he says the words makes me pause. "Do you...know what they were? Her reasons for sending her family away? For never speaking to any of us again?"

There's a pause, a twinge in his shoulders—hardly noticeable—before he shakes his head. "Of course not. I was just a kid then, too. But I trusted Vera, same as you."

That was my first mistake.

He spins around. "Look, I know I have no right to send people away from a home that's only half mine, but if she's going to be here, she can't disrespect my mom. Or you, for that matter. Can we at least agree on that?"

"Me? Really? You're the only one who can do that?"

He lowers two bowls from the cabinet, ignoring me, and prepares our dinner. All the camaraderie we shared moments ago is gone, and we've remembered who we are.

"I'm not all that hungry," I tell him as he places the bowl in my hand and turns off the stove.

"Suit yourself." He shrugs, moving past me and out of the room. Minutes later, I hear the door upstairs shut, telling me I'm alone.

CHAPTER SIX

BRIDGET

After dinner, I step outside and walk across the front porch, leaning up against the stone railing. The evening air is cool and quiet, except for the sounds of crickets and frogs singing from somewhere in the woods behind the house. Down beyond the gate, I can vaguely see the lights of the houses next door. It must be some of the women who were here before—the ones I don't know.

I'm not sure why it bothers me so badly that Cole knows things about Vera's life that I don't. Of course he does. He remained here, and I didn't. I still remember the day I moved into Bitter House—he was skinny as a rod back then, dark hair hanging into his eyes, that same cocky grin. I'd seen him around before, of course, during when I was younger, but I never thought much about him. He and Edna kept to themselves and gave our family plenty of space. After I moved into Bitter House, he'd lock himself in his room for hours listening to that stupid metal music that sounded like someone was screaming at him. He acted like I didn't exist, as if it was his house and I was the intruder.

Perhaps that's why this has triggered so many conflicting emotions for me now. In a way, not much has changed since I was the little girl with two dead parents moving into a house with people who didn't seem to want me there.

For the most part, Vera was locked away in her room, too, or traveling on some luxurious vacation that didn't allow children.

If it wasn't for Edna, I would've been alone in this big old house, filled with nothing but silence. She taught me how to braid my hair, how to play mancala. She introduced me to rom-coms and helped me with my school projects. I spent more time with her than her own son did, and yet she'd still choose him again and again. And so would Vera.

So *had* Vera, in fact. While I was kicked out at eighteen, Cole was allowed to stay here, and to come around in general, for much longer.

I'll never understand what was so wrong with me that no one wanted me around. That I was a burden and a nuisance to everyone who wasn't being paid to be kind to me.

A shiver runs over my body, and I turn back toward the house but stop short. On the mat is another letter, bent in the middle where it's clearly been stepped on.

I didn't notice it when I came outside. This envelope has no red ribbon around it, but it is marked clearly with a number one in the center. *The first of six secrets.*

I pick it up and tear it open this time, no longer trying to maintain the condition of the packaging. Inside the house, I lay the envelope down on the counter and open the folded letter.

The typed font is the same as the last one.

Bridget,

I'm sure by now you're questioning why you should trust me and, of course, who I must be. Don't worry. If you're still here, if you've stuck with me on this, you won't have to wait long for one of those answers. I'm going to earn your trust right now.

I have proof, you see. Proof that Vera Bitter was never the woman you thought you knew. She was a very good actress who never took off her mask, even for those who knew her best.

Vera Bitter was dangerous. She hurt people.

In her bedroom, there is a false wall in the back of her closet. Move it and you'll see what I mean.

Remember: whatever happens, don't make any decisions yet. There are more secrets to come soon.

Signed,
A friend

CHAPTER SEVEN

BRIDGET

My heart stalls as I read over the letter again. Is this really possible? A false wall in Vera's closet? It feels like something out of some Victorian folktale or a children's movie, not real life.

I'm somewhat concerned someone has a camera in there —*Cole*—and is planning to trick me into embarrassing myself.

Slowly, already regretting the decision, I head for the top floor, letter still in hand. When I reach it, I stop short at the sight waiting for me. Cole is standing at the top of a ladder, a tub of spackling paste resting on the ledge as he fills in what was apparently a hole near the top of the drywall.

I didn't even know we owned a ladder.

"What are you doing?"

He glances over his shoulder slowly, like he's not actually expecting to find anyone standing there, then jolts, a hand to his chest. The ladder shudders with the sudden movement, and once it's steady, he plucks an earbud from his ear. "Are you trying to give me a heart attack? What are you doing?"

"I wasn't trying to do anything. What exactly are you doing? Why do you have a ladder? Where did you *get* a ladder?"

He steps down, swiping the back of his hand over his forehead. "I'm fixing things. There was a crack in the wall that needed patching."

I stare up at the wall. "And that's your job?"

Anger flares in his eyes, but he quickly tamps it down. "I care about the house, Bridget. I don't want to see it fall apart. Is that really so hard for you to believe?"

"Believe, no. Understand, yes."

"It's mine—"

"Ours."

"One of the only things I've ever truly owned. It's the place where I grew up. Whether or not you wanted me here, this was where I spent my childhood. In a place where you made damn sure I felt like I didn't belong, it was all I had."

The sound that escapes his throat is basically a growl as he looks away from me, and my mouth goes dry. I'm not going to be made to feel bad about the way I treated him, not when he never treated me any better, but that doesn't mean I don't have empathy now. Still, it may have been the place he lived, but it wasn't his home.

In truth and fairness, it was never mine either.

"This house was Vera's, plain and simple. It never

belonged to anyone else after she moved in. Not you and not me. So we can spend our time arguing over things that don't really matter, or we can agree that this situation sucks. But we're in it together, and if we could just not kill each other in the process, that would be great."

"Fine by me." He shrugs.

"Fine." I zip past him and toward Vera's bedroom, remembering what I was actually trying to do before I got distracted. I reach her bedroom door—tall and made of dark wood. It had seemed so intimidating when I was a child. I'm flooded with memories of standing in this exact spot, the same hardwood floor underfoot that I feel beneath me now, trying to drum up the courage to knock and ask Vera for permission to go on the school's latest field trip or to give Edna the money to take me shopping for a dress for the winter formal. Standing before the door with a lump in my throat, preparing to tell her I was failing precalculus or I needed her to sign the test I didn't pass.

I push the door open, and I'm drowning in more memories. I never spent much time in Vera's room—it was always off limits—but the few times I was in here are burned into my memory.

The room is cool—always a few degrees colder than the rest of the house—and dark, and there's the distinct smell that's always been there. Her smell: jasmine and lilac, with a hint of body powder. I remember standing in her doorway talking to her while she dusted powder across her neck, plumes of white smoke floating all around her.

Swallowing, I walk past the vanity, the memories so real it's as if I can see her there. As if I can hear the tut of her tongue as she tells me to stand straighter, taller, prouder. As if I can feel her eyes narrowing on me, sizing me up.

The absence of her here is unnatural. This space belongs to her and her alone. Even if I planned to stay at Bitter House, I would never take over the master suite. It will never feel like it could belong to anyone but Vera.

Past her bed, laden with a large, mauve duvet and so many pillows it feels pretentious, is the doorway to her walk-in closet. The letter didn't say which wall is supposed to be false, so I start at the one closest to me, knocking on it cautiously.

It sounds...like a wall. I'm not exactly sure what I'm looking for.

Should it sound hollow?

A vague memory flashes through my mind, of my father knocking on our walls to find the stud before hanging something heavy.

"Hear that difference, B?" he'd asked, and I'd nodded, wanting to impress him, though I couldn't actually hear any difference at all.

Memories of my parents are rare. I was days away from turning ten when we were involved in the crash that stole them from me, so it's not like I don't have memories with them, just that most of the memories are sort of blocked, I guess. Like they're there—the way my mother laughed, the smell of my dad's aftershave, the sounds of them moving through the house, their voices—but everything is sort of hidden behind a fog. A dusty window that I can just barely manage to clean enough to peek through.

Clear memories like the one I've just had are exceptionally rare, and each time they happen, it's as if I'm losing them all over again. I claw at the memory, trying to keep it with me, to study his face, replay his voice, but it's gone. Smoke that slips through my bare fingers in an instant.

Blinking to clear my dry eyes, I nudge Vera's clothes to the side, being smacked by another wave of her signature perfume as I do. There's a bottle of it on the large dressing table in her closet behind me, and without looking, I can see it. Clear bottle, golden liquid inside. I used to think it was so elegant the way she'd spray her pulse points so gently, as if she were painting a canvas.

Looking back, so much of my experience with my grandmother is just me being in awe of her. I watched her move like a movie star and admired her as if I were an adoring fan. And that's how it always felt. She was the star I watched on the screen of a television. I could stand so close to her but never actually touch her, never reach her in any meaningful way.

With Vera's clothing moved aside, I have access to the back wall. I lean against it and knock on it cautiously, trying to decide if it sounds any different than the wall before it.

"What are you doing?"

I jump back as if the wall is on fire to find Cole standing behind me, both hands in his pockets as he stares at me with one dark brow quirked.

"Nothing. I thought you were working."

"I was." He shrugs. "Now I'm trying to decide if we need to take you to the hospital because you've obviously lost your mind."

I scowl. "I'm fine."

"Clearly." He gestures around the closet. "Perfectly normal to be listening to walls."

Pulling the letter from my back pocket, I pass it to him with a groan. "If you must know, I'm...trying to decide if these letters are serious."

He reads over it, his dark eyes zipping from one line to the next, and when he looks up, all traces of the smile previously there have been washed away from his mouth.

"When did you find this?"

"A few minutes ago."

His eyes flick to the wall behind me. "And you think there's something behind the wall."

"Only one way to find out."

He walks past me, cautiously, moving as if he thinks he's being pranked. As he nears the wall, he gives me an uncertain look and leans down, pressing his ear to the drywall as he raps against it. Then, an inch to the right. Farther down. Back to the left.

He scours the wall, searching left and right, up and down with his ear to it, knuckles knocking every few inches.

He's down near the bottom of the wall, knees in between two pairs of Vera's favorite boots, when he stops. Knocks again. His eyes light up, and he looks at me.

"What is it? Did you find something?"

He leans back on his heels, studying the wall. "I'm not sure, but it sounds..." His voice trails off as he presses in on the wall in the space where his ear was just placed. There's nothing on the wall to indicate anything abnormal. To my eyes, it looks exactly like the rest of the space.

At first, he doesn't seem to press hard enough because nothing happens, but when he tries again, a piece of the wall caves in, opening at the bottom like a door on a hinge. The rectangular piece is about a foot wide and six inches tall. It leans back with the pressure he's applying, and when he releases, it bounces forward in an instant, as if it's on a spring.

His eyes lift to mine, jaw slack, and for a moment, time stands still.

What is happening?

Until this moment, I'm not sure I actually expected us to find anything. For this to work.

"The letter was right..." I whisper, dropping to my knees next to him and picking it up from where he placed it on the floor. "Do you see anything? Is there anything behind there?"

Slowly, he pushes the wall in again, harder this time, and I see the faint edge of what looks like an open drawer underneath it. Shadows hide anything inside until Cole uses his free hand to pull his phone from his pocket and shines the light into the darkness.

He jerks his hand back at the same time as I gasp.

Our eyes meet, both of us confused by what we just saw.

Drawing in a deep breath, he pushes the piece of wall back once more and eases his hand down into the drawer, retrieving the black metal and holding it out as if it were a snake.

His eyes meet mine again. "Did you know Vera had a gun?"

CHAPTER EIGHT

BRIDGET

With a lump in my throat, I stare at the handgun resting in Cole's palm. What use could my prim and proper and perfectly put together grandmother have for a handgun hidden in a false wall in her closet?

Lots of people have guns, I try to reason with myself. *This doesn't prove anything. It doesn't make her dangerous.*

I swallow and stand, running my hands over my thighs. "Put it back." My voice is barely above a whisper, but Cole does as I've instructed him to, sliding the gun back in place and standing up. He runs a hand through his raven hair. "You didn't know that was in there?"

"Maybe it wasn't hers," I say softly, talking to myself more than him. "Maybe it was my grandfather's. Maybe she didn't know about it. Even if it was hers, so what? It proves nothing."

"It might not have been hers, sure." He pinches his

bottom lip between his thumb and forefinger. "But regardless of whose it was, how would whoever wrote this letter have known about it? Why would they think it means she's dangerous? Maybe she just had it for protection. She was a wealthy woman living relatively alone. She had employees and us, of course, but it would've been up to her to protect the house."

I nod. It makes sense. It's not as if finding a gun in the house is too much of a reason to be afraid, but it feels so out of place here. It's as if I've been doused with ice water in the middle of the street. Everything feels wrong. Off.

"She was by herself," I repeat, mostly to myself. "It was probably just for protection. Whoever wrote the note is just trying to scare us, like with the lock-your-door thing before." I pause, chewing the inside of my cheek. "But you're right, who else would've known about the gun?" My eyes find his. "Your mom?"

"Maybe," he mutters, "or..." He pauses. Swallows.

"*Or?*"

"There was..." He pauses again, rubbing a hand over his mouth.

"Spit it out, Cole."

"I'm trying to remember. There was...this night right after you moved in. Maybe a month or so after. I came down in the middle of the night to get a snack and"—his brows pinch together as he clearly tries to piece together the memory—"there was a man in the kitchen. They were fighting. Like...arguing."

"A man? *Who?*" I don't understand. In all my time

coming to Bitter House after my grandfather died, even before I'd moved in, I never knew Vera to have any men over, aside from my cousins—Zach and Jonah—and their dad—my uncle Marcus, who works overseas and is only around on holidays. Zach and Jonah would have both been kids back then, hardly men.

"I don't know. An older man. He was shouting at her, and...I think she had a gun."

My throat goes dry. "Wait. *What?* What are you talking about? You're just remembering this now?"

He massages the bridge of his nose with his eyes closed. "I don't know for sure that I'm even remembering it right. It was a long time ago, and *if* she had a gun, I never saw it. Her back was to me when I walked into the room, and she wasn't, like, holding him at gunpoint or anything." His eyes open, then he squeezes them shut again. "I just remember him asking something like 'what are you going to do, shoot me?' But then I walked into the room, and they saw me. Realized I was there. He stepped away from her, and Vera told me to go back upstairs."

"And you just left her?" I demand. Granted, he would've been about twelve at the time, if it was right after I moved in, but he could've told someone, woken his mom, called the police, *something*.

"Of course not." He scowls. "I walked into the room and asked what was going on, but Vera told me to go to bed again, so I went and woke up Mom."

"And then what happened?"

He sighs. "I don't remember. She told me to go to sleep

and she would handle it, and I never heard anything else. I didn't really think anything else about it until now. But if she had a gun that night, if she was hiding it from me, that man—whoever he was—would've known about it."

"And you've never seen him again?"

"I don't think so, no."

"But, even if he knew she owned a gun, would he have known where it was hidden?"

He sighs, scrubbing his hand over his head. "I guess there's not really a way to know."

"I don't understand. Why didn't you tell me about all of this when it happened?"

His brows pinch together, his chestnut eyes drilling into me as if I'm ridiculous. "It's not like we were friends back then. You hated me."

"I didn't hate you. I...you were mean to me. I moved in here because my parents had died. I was scared and alone and sad, and you acted like having to share a house with me was a punishment."

"It wasn't that." He sighs, weighing his words. "It was...I already felt out of place here, and then you came along—Vera's *actual* family—and it made me feel like I was even more invisible. Suddenly my mom had this new kid to take care of, and her job was busier than ever. I didn't even know you when you moved in. It was never about you. I was actually excited to have someone my age here at first, until I realized it meant the time I had with my mom and Vera was split. And then I tried to get to know you, and you acted like you were too good for me.

Like you were disgusted to share a house with *me*, and I thought—"

"Yeah, right. I specifically remember *you* calling *me* a 'Goody-Two-Shoes' a few days after I'd moved in. Before I'd done anything to possibly make you mad."

He waves a hand in my direction, gesturing up and down my body. "Please. You were the perfect, shiny little rich kid who spent hours in the bathroom doing her hair and picking out her clothes. And, if I'm remembering it right, I called you that *after* you were rude to my friends when I had them over."

"Because your friends were idiots."

He looks like he's going to argue, but he thinks better of it and nods. "Fair, but the point is I avoided you because it was clear you'd rather not be around me."

I press my lips together. I could argue or lie, but the truth is, he's right. I didn't want to be around Cole back then because he was a constant reminder that some people still had a mother. Every time he fought with Edna or slammed his door, every time he argued with her over something stupid, I wanted to tell him how lucky he was. How he should just hug her because she could be gone in a split second.

But I was a kid, and he was an older boy who wanted nothing to do with me, so I kept my mouth shut and seethed in silence.

He folds his arms across his chest and draws in a deep breath. "I'm sorry about how I treated you back then, okay? I am. And I'm not saying we have to be friends, but can we at least try to get along for the sake of figuring out what's going on?"

I nod with a deep breath of my own. "Yeah, okay."

"Great." He holds out his hand and shakes mine like this is some sort of business deal, and then we walk from the room, leaving Vera's secret hidden in the wall.

CHAPTER NINE

BRIDGET

A faint buzzing sound draws me from sleep, and I roll over, rubbing my eyes and praying it will stop.

It doesn't.

Or rather, it does, and then it immediately starts up again.

I groan and reach for my phone, blinking sleep from my eyes as I stare at the screen, trying to decipher the words on it.

Ana

My best friend. I've been meaning to call her and update her on things, but the days have gotten away from me. I swipe my thumb across the screen and touch the button to put it on speaker, dropping the phone onto my stomach as I roll onto my back.

"Hello?" I rub sleep from my eyes.

"Ah-ha! She lives!" The deep voice she's using is something between a swamp creature and Darth Vader.

Returning to her normal voice, she adds, "And here I was, preparing to send a search party."

I chuckle. "I know. I'm sorry. I planned to call you, but things have been so weird."

"Uh-oh. Weird how? Is everything okay?"

"Yeah, it's fine, I just..." I debate telling her about the letters, but with the sudden strange desire to protect Vera, I change my mind. Thankfully, that isn't the only weird thing to happen lately. "Actually, since I arrived, I found out I'm not the only one the house was left to."

"What do you mean?" Her mouth sounds full when she asks, and I can tell she's eating breakfast—probably a cinnamon roll, which is her current obsession.

"Vera left it to me and Cole."

"Cole?" There's a pause, then she gasps. "Wait. Cole your, like, ex-stepbrother?"

"No. Or, well, yes, but we aren't stepsiblings. He just lived here because his mom worked for Vera and lived at Bitter House, too."

"I thought you two didn't get along."

I sit up in bed, stretching and running a hand through my messy hair. "Bingo. We don't. Which has made this all a bit more interesting, to say the least."

She sucks in a breath. "I don't get it. Your grandmother left her house to both of you? Why would she do that? Do you think she's just trying to mess with you?"

"I really don't know. I wouldn't put anything past Vera, but this feels especially cruel."

She clicks her tongue, thinking. "So, what? Can you just sell the house? Or buy him out? What's the plan?"

"I don't have the money to buy him out, even if I wanted to. The good news is he doesn't either, so I don't have to worry about that, but I don't know if I want to sell. I mean, I have no idea if I'd ever really move back here, but it's a huge house." I mimic Vera's deep, matronly voice. "*A manor.*" She snorts at my impression. "Seriously, it's not like I could ever afford anything like this now."

"You could if you sell," she points out.

"And split the profits," I remind her.

"Oh. Right." She sighs. "Well, what does he think about it? Do you know what he wants to do?"

"We're kind of dancing around the subject right now, waiting for everything to get settled with the court. We talked about using the house like a vacation spot we could split."

"I'm assuming you'd want to check in with each other though, so you don't, like, walk in on him doing it with someone on the kitchen table." It's impossible, but I can practically hear her wincing. "And you should probably hire a cleaner for the same reason. Give them specific instructions to bleach everything." She chuckles, but I barely hear it, as a hard knot has formed in my stomach at the thought of Cole and another woman in this house. She's right—if we split it, there's a chance that will be part of it. Eventually, he'll get married, have kids, and so will I.

But before that, there will likely be dates and romantic

69

getaways I might interrupt. We'd have to come up with some sort of system.

I flash back to the many girls he had over when we were in high school, and I push away the memories. It doesn't matter to me what Cole does, as long as he doesn't bother me or destroy the house.

"Yeah, I guess so," I say eventually, realizing she's still waiting for a response. "Anyway, for now, it looks like I'm going to have to stay here. At least for a little while longer than I'd originally planned to. I haven't had a chance to talk to Jenna about it, but my goal is to ask about working from here as much as possible until things are settled."

"How long do you think that will take?"

I rub my lips together, wishing I had a clearer answer. "I'm not sure how long the court stuff will take, but we're working on getting the house fixed up and dealing with family drama on top of everything else, so it's all kind of a disaster."

"Family drama? What do you mean? From Vera?"

"No, just my aunt. Basically, everyone is upset over what they were given in the will, and they're coming after me over it as if I had anything to do with what Vera chose to do."

"Yikes. No offense, girl, but your grandma seems like she was trying to start drama with her last act."

"Honestly, I can't see Vera caring enough to do that, but maybe. It's all just a mess." I huff, running a hand over my face. Until this moment, I'm not sure I realized how stressed this situation has me.

"Do you need me to come up there? I can get a few days off work."

"Thanks, but I'm okay for now." I don't want anyone outside of this messed-up world to see it from the inside, no matter how much I trust Ana. "I think Jenna would lose her mind if we were both out of the office. But I may still take you up on the offer to help move things out of here once I decide what I want to take."

"Yeah, of course. Name the time and place, and I'm there. And don't worry about Jenna, okay? She'd handle it. I could bring my laptop with me and work from there. You're already working remotely and things are going fine, aren't they?"

"In theory." Meaning, I have several unread emails waiting for me and haven't opened my latest spreadsheet since I arrived.

"We could totally make it work, then. We'd just work during the day and pack at night. Teamwork." She giggles.

"Maybe. I'll let you know, okay?"

She huffs. "Yeah, for sure. Just promise me you'll let me know if I can help you, whether it's from there or from here. You don't have to do this all on your own. I got you, girl. You know that, right?"

"I do know," I promise her. "And thank you. Give Teddy and Olivia kisses from me."

"Will do. They miss you, B. We all do."

"I miss you guys, too. I promise I'll be home as soon as I can." I only hope I can keep that promise.

"Okay, I'll let you go back to the current soap opera

you're living in." The sound of water running comes across her line, and I assume she's rinsing the plate she was just eating off of. "Call me, though, okay? Check in so I know you're still alive."

"I will."

"Love you, lady."

"Love you."

I press the button to end the call and place my phone back on the nightstand before crossing the room to get ready for the day. Once I've showered and changed, I make my way downstairs, passing Cole's closed door.

At the bottom of the stairs, a sound catches my attention.

Someone is knocking on the door.

I hesitate at the door, peeking out the window next to it and recognize the face immediately, a groan escaping my lips.

I pull the door open, staring into the face of the realtor from yesterday. "How do you keep getting through the gate?" I demand.

"I have the code." He flashes me a smile.

"How?" Did Cole lie? He told me he let him in before, not that he'd had a code.

"Someone gave it to me." Another of those charming smiles that has probably gotten him inside a lot of doors. Not this one. I move my body to block more of the doorway.

"Who would've done that? Cole?"

"Not a chance." The voice comes from behind me, and I glance over my shoulder to find Cole standing in the hallway, hair messy from sleep. He stalks toward me, eyes trained on the man. "Can we help you? We made it clear yesterday you weren't needed."

The man straightens his stance, shoving his hands into his pockets. "I was hoping you'd reconsider. Let me tell you, I've run some comps..." He whistles. "You two are sitting on a goldmine here."

"Not interested." Cole locks his jaw, gripping the door. "You should go."

Something about the way the man twists his lips catches my eyes, and my heart stops. There's something familiar about him I didn't notice before. His lips crack into a wry, lifeless smile, and my chest constricts.

He looks just like his mother.

Noticing, Cole looks down at me.

"Zach." I mutter the word, breathless. I haven't seen my cousin since he was a child, but there's no doubt in my mind that's who this is, all grown up and trying his hardest to get our grandmother's house from me. No doubt his mother is in on this.

His eyes flash to me, a hint of bitterness in them, but he plasters on the smile again. "Okay. Yeah, you caught me. Good to see you again, cousin."

Cole turns his attention back to the door. "You lied to me yesterday."

Zach shakes his head. "I didn't lie, I just didn't tell you my name."

"You told me someone called you. You told me *Bridget* called you."

The smile warps from his face. "Right. Okay, technically that was a lie, but I knew if you realized who I was, you'd kick me out before you heard what I had to say."

"Look at that, B, he's a fortune teller." Cole moves to shut the door, but Zach catches it.

"Hear me out. Please. I just want to talk. My mom is devastated about not getting Bitter House. This place is all she has left of her mother." His blue eyes find mine. "Surely you, of all people, understand that."

My breathing catches because *of course* I understand that. Am I wrong for keeping the house away from Aunt Jenn? Does she really deserve it more than I do? Even if she does, it's not like the decision is solely mine.

Though...the idea of her sharing the house with Cole is pretty amusing.

"Don't do that." Cole steps in front of me. "Don't guilt-trip her. She was given the house because it's what Vera wanted. I'm sure the millions she left you will buy you something equally as nice."

"I can speak for myself." I nudge Cole out of the way. "He's right, though. This was Vera's choice. I have to believe she wanted me to have the house for a reason."

"She knew you wouldn't sell it," Cole says. "And they would. This house meant everything to her."

Zach swallows, and I watch anger overtake his features—wrinkling, dimpling, darkening. "Vera was an old bitch who hated everyone around her. Who cares what mattered to her? She loved this house more than she loved her family."

I flinch at the harsh tone of his voice. "Look, you should

go. Like I told your mom yesterday...feel free to take this up with the lawyers. I'm not selling the house. And you can tell your brother the same thing before he tries to sneak over here."

"My brother is in Shenzhen with my dad. There's no reason we can't handle this ourselves. Name your price."

Cole nods toward the driveway, starting to close the door. "You should go."

Zach curses under his breath, stepping back with a frustrated wave in our direction, as if he's batting us away. "Call me when you change your mind."

"We won't," Cole says. He shuts the door and crosses the room quickly on his way through the living room.

I double-check the lock before following him. When I find him in the kitchen, he's staring into space as if he's seen a ghost.

"What's wrong?"

"I need to tell you something. I don't know if it means anything, but...you should know."

"Tell me what?"

"Vera and Zach were fighting before she died." He blurts the words out as if they were lava on his tongue.

"Fighting?"

"Arguing about something, yeah. I remember Mom talking about it, about Vera being upset. I never thought anything about it because it didn't seem like a big deal, and it happened like three or so months before she died, but now with them trying to force their way into the house..." He pauses, running a hand through his hair. "What if there's a reason they want this house so badly? What if they're the ones writing the letters? Trying to scare us away?"

"Call your mom." I can hardly muster the words.

"What?" Cole stares at me.

"I want to hear it from her. Better yet, ask her to come here. She has to know more than she's told us, and it's time we got to the bottom of it."

"You want her to come here?"

"Yeah. We need to ask her about the man Vera was fighting with the night you overheard them, and I want to know about Zach." I don't say the rest, but the truth is, I want to know the truth about everything. Why Vera kicked me out, why there was a rift in the family in the first place, why Vera would've left the house to the two of us, and I need to see Edna's face, to search for hints she might be lying when she gives us the answers.

"Okay. Sure. I'll see if she's busy."

CHAPTER TEN

BRIDGET

Three hours later, we've had breakfast and are waiting impatiently when Edna arrives at the house. She looks just like I remember—graying, blonde hair cut short around her head, her warm, silver eyes matching her gray eyeshadow almost perfectly.

We find her at the door with arms loaded with grocery bags.

"You didn't have to bring us anything," Cole says, hurrying to take the bags from her arms as he kisses her cheek.

"I know, I know." She hands them off without a fuss. "But I know how the two of you like to eat." She winks at me, but there's a hint of sadness I hadn't expected. The moment is heavy. It's been so long since I last saw the woman I considered to be a mother figure. The woman I trusted more than anyone else for most of my life. Her shoulders rise with a deep breath, and she holds her hands out to her sides, waiting to see if I'll accept her hug. "Bridget."

In the end, it's not really a question. No matter how conflicted my feelings are about Edna, she's the last mother figure I have left. I hug her back, squeezing for an extra long time as I breathe the scent of her citrus perfume.

I've missed her.

The thought cracks me open. I've missed her so much it hurts. And I'm angry with her. And hurt. And somehow, that all fits inside of me like a neatly packed suitcase.

"It's good to see you back here," she says softly, cupping my cheek with her hand.

"It's...strange...to be back," I admit. "Thank you for the groceries. You really didn't have to do that."

"Yeah, well, old habits die hard. What can I say? I miss making the weekly grocery run for this place."

There's no mistaking the way her voice cracks as she says it. I guess I never really thought about how much it might hurt Edna to leave this house. It was her home for longer than it was mine, and Vera seemed to be her friend. It's more proof that Vera was a friend to no one—that she left Edna nothing.

"Well, you're welcome to come back and help us out," Cole teases. "We haven't turned your old room into a theater just yet."

She purses her lips at him.

"I'm serious, this place is much nicer than my apartment. I've told you a million times you didn't have to leave."

His eyes slowly lift toward mine. "As long as my roomie agrees."

I open my mouth. The idea of being here with the two of them, of being outnumbered, makes my stomach churn with a sensation I don't quite recognize. Would it be better or worse to have Edna here? "Oh, I—"

Before I can say anything, Edna is shaking her head. "I've told you. I never wanted to stay here after Vera passed. It's too hard to be here without her. I need to move on. We *all* need to move on." Her eyes travel the room with a nostalgic gleam before she shakes her head, blinking back tears, and clears her throat. "Well..." She sighs, running her hands over her hips. "Cole says you've gotten some letters you want me to take a look at."

I nod. "That, among other things."

"Let's take a look." Despite my initial hesitations and worry over seeing her again, just her presence in this house has calmed me, soothed my nerves like a balm. She makes me feel safe, like she always did as a kid. Even now, I feel better knowing that a *real* adult is here to help sort this out. I wonder how old you have to be before you stop feeling that way?

We make our way into the kitchen where I have laid out the two letters, and Edna picks one up, holding it carefully. I can't help noticing the way her hands have aged, now wrinkled and with knuckles swollen from arthritis. At first glance, she was every bit the woman I once knew, but upon closer inspection, I see the loose skin around her jaw, the wrinkles in the corners of her eyes—proof she's been given the privilege of aging, unlike my parents.

I'll never be able to look at aging as something to avoid or escape. For me, as I inch closer to the age my parents were when they died, I know every day is something to be grateful for.

She reads over the first letter, then the second, before placing them down. Her lips form a hard line, and she leans against the island, resting her chin against her fist.

"And you have no idea where the letters are coming from?"

"No. They've been left on the front porch both times. It has to be someone who knows the gate code," I tell her.

She nods. "Yes, but that could be a lot of people. Vera hasn't changed it in years. There were so many delivery drivers and service men, ex-employees. It doesn't help."

"We found a gun in the wall, just like the letter said," Cole tells her. "Did you know it was there?"

I'm expecting her to say no, so when she nods hesitantly, chills creep and crawl over my skin like cobwebs.

"I knew Vera kept a gun in the house, yes." She looks at me. "It was your grandfather's. She kept it hidden so you kids would never find it, but it was just the two of us here, two women. If someone came in and tried to hurt us, Vera wanted to be prepared."

I nod, though I still can't imagine Vera ever harming anyone. Not physically, anyway. No, she preferred to break spirits, not bones.

"And the rest of it? The secrets?" I gesture toward the

notes. "The fact that she was dangerous? What do you think? Do you have any idea what they could be talking about? Cole says you mentioned she was fighting with Zach before she died. And that there was an incident with a man yelling at her in the kitchen a few months after I moved in."

She nods, running a hand over her stomach with a deep inhale. "Why don't we all sit down?"

Agreeing, I follow her into the sitting room and take a seat on the sofa. Cole sits next to me and Edna takes the armchair, scooting it until it's directly in front of us. This is eerily reminiscent of the many times Edna lectured us about grades or parties or safe sex from these exact spots.

"To answer your first question, yes. Vera and Zach weren't seeing eye to eye in the months before she died, but that wasn't unusual. Before Vera died, when her health was declining, Zach reached out to ask about her will. Vera was adamant she didn't want anyone except her attorneys to know what was in it until she'd died. She used witnesses provided by the firm and wouldn't let anyone else know what it held. Of course, your aunt wasn't happy about that, and Zach made it known."

I rub my lips together, thinking. "I don't understand, though. I thought they hadn't had contact in years."

Edna takes a deep breath, eyes drifting toward the ceiling with a shake of her head. "Well, if it had been up to Vera, they wouldn't have. She cut them off, but Jennifer isn't one to let things go, as you're probably going to find out. She always thought Vera should be doing more for her boys. She thought she was favoring you, that you got special treatment because you lived with Vera."

If she only knew.

Edna wrings her hands together in her lap. "When Vera sent them all away, it wasn't the last she heard from Jennifer, and as the boys got older, they started calling, too. Sending letters, coming to the house and even, a few times, tracking her down and confronting her in public to ask for money for this or that."

"And did she give them anything?" A lump forms in my throat.

"Never."

"But why? Why send them away and refuse to help them? I never understood that. Vera had plenty of money." We both seem to know I'm not only asking about Aunt Jenn and my cousins. "Why would she abandon them?"

Edna sighs, her eyes wide with worry and frustration. "Vera had her reasons. I know you think she was cold. I know you think what she did to you—sending you away— was awful, and I'm inclined to agree with you." She pats my thigh. "But, sweetheart, she loved you. In the only way she knew how, she loved you. She was complicated and... distant." She's clearly choosing her words carefully. "But she wasn't a bad person." She glances back into the kitchen. "Whatever those letters say, whoever is sending them, don't let them tarnish the good memories you have with your grandmother."

"I don't know that I had any good memories," I admit.

"That's not true. She took you in. She gave you everything you could want."

"That wasn't love. She wasn't the one taking me to doctor's appointments when I was sick. She wasn't the one taking me shopping for clothes before each new school year. Or talking me through my first breakup."

"She paid for those things, Bridget. Gave me the time away from my work to be able to help you through everything. I know you can't understand it, but Vera was here for you in the only way she knew how to be."

I inhale deeply. "You're right, I don't understand that. I never will. How can you defend her? You were always here for me, and then you just took her side in the end, just packed my bags and sent me on my way." My voice cracks, and humiliation fills me as tears overflow from my eyes. I didn't want to do this.

"Sweetheart..." She brushes my tears away, and just like that, I'm twelve years old, with Edna holding me against her chest while I sob over a nightmare about the car crash once again. "It was never about sides. Is that what you've thought all these years? Following Vera's orders never meant I loved you any less. I begged her not to go through with it, but her mind was made up. I did what I had to do, but it never meant I stopped checking up on you or worrying about you." She smiles through tears of her own. "I love you like you are my own child. As much as I love my own child." Her eyes find Cole.

He clears his throat. "What about the man in the kitchen that night? Do you remember him?"

"Vera always tried to keep her private life private," she says, drying her eyes. "That night, it didn't work. The man you saw was an old friend who'd had too much to drink. A simple misunderstanding."

"Who was it?" I ask.

"No one you know. I don't want you to worry about it. It was hard for Vera to date, you understand, being who she was. Wealthy, well known. But that didn't mean she never got lonely. Sometimes men misunderstood her intentions."

I swallow. The idea of Vera dating feels impossible. She hid so much of herself from me, but I never imagined a whole part of her daily life could be concealed.

"Tell me. Have you kids talked about selling the house?" Edna asks, running her hands over her legs.

"Jenn and Zach want us to," I admit.

"They've been here?" Her eyes widen.

"Both of them, yeah."

"They're never going to let it go." She sighs. "Maybe you should sell. To them or someone else. And get away. From this. From everything."

"You really think so?" Cole asks, his voice hitching with the surprise that I feel.

Edna doesn't answer for a while, but eventually, she says, "I know better than anyone what a complicated person Vera was. I have no idea why she wanted you to have this house, and I'm trying to respect her wishes, but I also need to look out for the both of you. If being here isn't what makes you happy, sell. These are your lives to live. Vera can't control them anymore."

There is no malice in her voice, only sadness. Longing that I really don't understand.

"Why did you stay for so long?" I ask her. "She was cold to you as well. Didn't you ever think about finding another job?"

"As a person, Vera was...complex, but she was also my best friend." Tears well in her eyes. "I loved her with everything I had. She gave me a home. A job. Despite everything, she was the closest thing I ever had to a sister. We loved each other in a way that's hard to explain. We...we understood each other. And she didn't always have it easy, you know. After your grandfather died." She studies me, begging me to understand like she always has. But back then, she was asking me to forgive her for hurting other people—my aunt, my cousins. Now, it's me Vera has hurt, and I'm not sure how I'll ever forgive her for that.

"Your experience with Vera wasn't mine," I say, carefully picking the words as I go. "I know I don't know everything about her, but someone does. And I'm not leaving this house until I learn the truth."

CHAPTER ELEVEN

BRIDGET

After a few hours, Edna leaves and I find myself wandering down the hall and back toward Vera's bedroom. Everything Edna said rings through my head in faded whispers. There's so much about Vera that I don't know. So much I'll never be able to understand.

In her closet, there are sets of photo albums. When I first moved to Bitter House, she allowed me to look through them on occasion, to see photos of my mother when she was growing up. Everything seemed different then, when my mother was alive. My grandfather.

Vera was different. In the years when my grandfather was still alive, she seemed so full of life. There are photographs of the family—Vera and Harold and my mom and Aunt Jenn at the park, on the sofa downstairs in the sitting room, playing in the yard. Everything sparked with a light that just wasn't present in my earliest memories of my grandmother.

She was a different person.

I wish I could've known who she was before.

I know this house used to belong to my grandfather's family, before he married Vera, and I know they inherited it when his parents died. Though Vera never talked about that time with me, I know they were happy from the photographs. I don't think you can fake that sort of thing. When my mom talked about her parents, it was always fondly. She had a happy childhood, and as I smile down at the face of the toddler she once was, I'm so grateful for that.

I'm grateful she never had to live with the same woman who raised me.

After Harold died, Vera married another man. I don't know if I ever knew his name until I read the obituary. It was after my mom moved out of the house, and it doesn't seem like she ever knew him very well. I get the feeling it was some sort of quickie-Vegas wedding that was quickly annulled so he didn't get his hands on the fortune Harold left behind for Vera, but that's purely the story I've formed in my mind.

"You okay?"

I look over at Cole's legs, then up toward his face. He's holding two stemless wine glasses with a fizzy, slightly green-tinted liquid in them.

"Just looking at pictures." In the one on top, Vera is sitting on the bench of a speedboat, a sun hat tied to her head with her daughters on either side of her. The smile on her face is so unrecognizable, it's as if I'm staring at a stranger.

"I thought you could use a drink." He sits down next to

me, handing one of the glasses over. "Do you mind the company?"

I sniff the drink, and he laughs.

"It's not poisoned, don't worry. I'll trade you, if you want."

I hold it out. "Actually, yeah."

He rolls his eyes playfully but takes it in stride and switches our glasses.

I take a sip. Vodka soda with extra lime juice. One of my favorites, though he couldn't possibly know that, and I'm pretty sure it was Edna's favorite, too.

"She was so different back then," I say, running a finger over the photograph. "We didn't get to see this version of her."

"Life changes you," he says sadly. "Losing people. Parents, grandparents, siblings, aunts, uncles, a husband, a daughter and son-in-law. Nearly everyone she ever loved was gone long before she was. I don't know how she was still standing, if I'm being honest."

I flip to the next photograph, grinning when I see my mother dressed in a very large prom dress next to a boy her age, while my grandfather looks on from the background. This must've been taken just before he died. They had no idea it was coming.

There are several photographs of Vera and my grandfather at various outings, galas, and parties, always dressed in the finest formalwear and looking better than everyone around them.

"They certainly were something, weren't they?" I muse,

taking a sip of my drink and glancing at Cole next to me. We're so close our shoulders are practically touching.

"What do you think it's like?" he asks, his voice low and curious. "To love someone that much?"

I look up to meet his eyes, shocked by the question. His gaze lifts from the photo and back to me, his dark eyes warmer than I think I've ever seen them.

A current swims through my core. "I wouldn't know," I say softly. "Cozy, I guess. Safe."

"I feel like it's the opposite," he whispers, his eyes drilling into mine. He cocks his head to the side, looking away briefly, and I miss the way he was just looking at me, miss the heat of his gaze. He pulls his knee up, bending his leg under himself, and his pants brush my thigh. My mind goes slightly fuzzy at the contact, and I look down, waiting to see if he's going to pull away.

When I look back over at him, his eyes are there waiting for me. His throat swells with a swallow that I feel somewhere deep inside of me.

The air is thick between us with something like anxiety on fire. Suddenly, the space around us is too small, and we're too close. I can feel his body heat. Or...no. Maybe that's mine. My face is hot, ears ringing. I should want to pull away from him, but I don't.

If anything, I want to be closer.

What is happening to me? This is Cole. *Cole!* The man I've loathed my entire life, but suddenly, it doesn't feel so much like loathing. It feels...like the static electricity on clothes when you pull them from the dryer.

Tension crackles through the air between us, and my breathing slows.

"The opposite?" I ask.

His Adam's apple bobs with another hard swallow, and he looks away from me, down into his glass. Swirling the cup in his hand, he says, "It must be terrifying, I mean. To love someone so much when you know you'll lose them someday. And then..." His eyes bounce back up to mine. "And then you'll never be the same."

I swallow. "I guess you're right."

"Have you ever been in love, B? *Bridget?*" He corrects himself quickly.

"You can call me B." I'm trying to buy myself time more than anything because I feel like I might combust. These feelings have never been here between the two of us. "And, um, yeah. Once." I chew my bottom lip. "In college." I lift my glass to my mouth, breaking whatever spell I'm currently under as I take another sip. "Blake Potter."

His eyes follow my glass from my lips and back down, and there's that magic again. My heart is racing in my chest, clawing at my ribcage. "What happened?"

"It just...didn't, um, work out," I say, my voice low and slow. It's taking real concentration to make my brain work. He licks his lips, and I follow his tongue with my gaze, trying to make the words in my head string together to form a coherent sentence. "We, um, we...dated for three out of the four years and then it just sort of fizzled out when we realized we both wanted different things. Like...I wanted to start a career, plan a life, and...he wanted to backpack through

Europe and *find himself*." Even now, my smile is bitter, but the pain is numb. Cole scoots a bit closer to me, and the cologne on his skin ignites my senses.

"I'm sorry." He seems genuine when he says it.

I shake his concern off as his eyes dance between mine. He looks as if he might kiss me, and I think I might be okay with it. "It was a long time ago." I look down, tucking a piece of hair behind my ears. What if this is all a trap? What if he's trying to seduce me and trick me into giving him the house? "What about you? Have you...been in love?" I can't bear to look at him as I ask.

"Um, I don't know."

The tension seems to dissipate as I look up at him, the lightning in the air nearly gone. I nudge him with my elbow. "Come on. I gave you a real answer." My skin rests against his for a moment too long, and he glances down at it, his cheeks growing red. Like a lit match to a room of gasoline, the fire is back.

"Once, too, I think. But it was a long time ago."

"And? What was her name?"

He looks away, one corner of his mouth upturned as he takes another big drink. "It doesn't matter."

"Why?" I'm desperate for the answer, ready to crawl out of my skin.

"It didn't work out." He shrugs.

"What happened?"

"We just...couldn't make it work. We were dumb kids."

"So, this was...in high school? Did I know her?" I run through the roster of girls he brought home.

He shakes his head, draining the rest of his glass. "Forget it, B. It's not a big deal. It wasn't love, anyway. It was just a crush."

I stand up, setting the photo album back in its place and chasing him across the room. Now the heat I feel is purely embarrassment. I was vulnerable with him, and he's telling me nothing. "Wait! That's not fair. I told you mine, you have to tell me yours. Did I know her? Was it one of the girls you used to bring here?"

He laughs without looking back. "No."

"Then who?"

Spinning on his heels so quickly I slam into him, sloshing the alcohol down both of our arms, he catches me, his hands on my waist, the touch so featherlight I almost don't feel him at all.

Except I do. I'm so incredibly aware of him, it seems impossible. The heat from his palms is searing me, but I don't want to pull away.

Why don't I want to pull away?

His gaze flicks to my lips, then back up. "You okay?"

His dark eyes once felt so empty, but now I see they're galaxies waiting to be explored. There's something deep and comforting about them, about the way he uses them and takes his time to rake his gaze over my body. There's a heat there that matches my own. "Why did you stop so quickly? You knew I was behind you."

"You shouldn't have been following me so closely." The corner of his mouth twitches.

"You shouldn't have been running away!" I squeeze his

arm, my fingers tingling from the connection. "Tell me who it was."

He rolls his eyes, dropping his hand away from me. "Oh my god, you're impossible. Let it go, B."

I drop my hand, too. "No. You asked the question, and now you're too embarrassed to tell the truth. Tell me who it was. I know her, don't I?"

He scrapes a hand through his hair. "I was making conversation. I didn't ask for you to go into detail. You chose to do that. It was a yes-or-no question, and I answered that. Just drop it, okay?"

I sigh, tossing my head back. I can't believe I let myself get so carried away. What I was feeling for Cole was not desire, it was the simmering disgust that has always been there. "Now I see why Vera left us the house. Clearly, she was hoping one of us would kill the other."

He grabs my hips without warning, pulling me flush against him. "To be clear..."

My body combusts, flames ripping through me, and I swear I have a headache from the whiplash going through my emotions right now. How is he doing this? He squeezes my hip, the other hand sliding across my collarbone, thumb against my neck. When his gaze falls to my lips, I give in to my desire. This is it. He's going to kiss me, and I'm going to let him.

He opens his mouth, and I feel his warm breath on my lips. I part them slowly, silently begging him to do it.

"I wouldn't kill you. Just seriously maim."

The words wash over me like a cool breeze, and he drops

his hands away from me, stepping back like I'm a flame that has just burned him.

"Phew," I mutter, my voice barely a whisper. "Good to know."

His eyes flash back to my lips again and then he's gone without another word. My heart beats so loudly in my ears I can't hear anything else.

When I make my way back down the stairs a few minutes later, the front door is standing open, and Cole is on the porch, another letter in hand. This envelope is marked with a number two, letting me know we're getting closer and closer to discovering the full truth.

"You found another one?" Any heat I felt moments ago is washed away in an instant.

"It was on the mat," he says, his eyes finding me with a strange bitterness. "I stepped out to get some...fresh air."

"We're going to have to install a camera," I tell him, the thought just now occurring to me. "And figure out how to change the gate code."

He nods, holding out the letter to me. "I'm assuming you want to be the first to read it."

I'm surprised by the gesture but take the envelope anyway, tearing it open. My eyes skim the familiar font, searching for the latest secret with trepidation.

Bridget,

If you're reading this, you found my last letter, and I'm

assuming you found Vera's secret too. I'm sorry to tell
you it's only going to get worse from here. I have
another secret to reveal, as promised, and another
thing for you to seek out. I wouldn't do this if I didn't
have to prove to you that I'm telling the truth about
everything.

Your grandmother wasn't just a liar.

She wasn't just a fraud.

She was also a murderer.

You'll find all the proof you need in the garden. That's
where the bodies are buried.

Signed,
A friend

PART 2

CHAPTER TWELVE

VERA BITTER

I was never sure about changing my last name after I was married. Isn't that funny? In those days especially, it was unheard of for a woman to think of such things.

But I was a Shuffle, had been all my life. My daddy was a Shuffle and his daddy and so on, and I guess, in some strange way, it felt like giving up the last piece of myself I had, if I chose to do it.

Harold would've allowed me to keep the name, if I wanted. That was the kind of man he was, you know? Kind and thoughtful. He really listened to me, and I know from talking to other women around town just how rare that is.

So, in the end, I took his name. I told him it was because I wanted my children to have the same last name as both their parents, but in reality, I think I did it because I loved him and wanted to make him happy.

And, if I'm being honest, I loved the weight the last name carried. Being a Bitter in this town, I might as well be a

Rockefeller or a Kennedy. Say the name, and suddenly tables open up, discounts are given, and people pop up to meet my every demand.

Harold was never the type of man to take advantage of that. He grew up with it, of course, so it was normal for him, but he tried not to let it get in his head. Me, on the other hand? I grew up with a mother who sliced already-sliced pieces of bread until they were thinner to make the loaves go further, who taught us broth could be a whole meal, and who split two cans of soup for dinner between the six of us. For me, power meant everything. It was a new concept, and frankly, I had a blast with it. Maybe too much, as Harold would sometimes point out once we were home, but he always said it with a hint of pride and that smile I'd grown to love so much.

I can still picture it now if I try. The way that smile made me feel could be studied. Entire books could be written about it. But...like all the best stories, it had to end.

And when it did, I was grateful I had the Bitter name. Because that's exactly what I was: bitter.

CHAPTER THIRTEEN

BRIDGET

I drop the letter onto the counter as if it's on fire, the contents of my stomach roiling with what I've just read. It's the same feeling I get whenever I watch true crime documentaries with Ana—sick and on edge. But this is worse. Whatever secrets Vera had, whoever she was, I refuse to believe she was a murderer. I refuse to believe she was capable of anything so atrocious.

But I have to know. I have to prove them wrong—this letter sender. Prove that they're trying to scare me, and it won't work.

"Why would they have mentioned the garden if they were lying?" Cole says when I tell him this theory. "It'll be easy enough to prove them wrong."

"Maybe they don't think we'll check. Maybe they think we'll be too scared."

"Only one way to find out," Cole says, walking past me with a determined look.

I follow him out of the house. It's getting dark already, the sunset painting the sky with watercolors in reds, purples, and oranges. It's eerily quiet out here; the only sound is the swishing of our shoes across the grass.

My throat is dry as we reach the garden, and I stare down. Vera was always so proud of her flower garden. The few times I can remember seeing her smile, it was always here. She'd sit on the concrete bench in the center of the square garden, surrounded by flowers of every color and variety, and just...relax. It was rare for her, someone who always seemed to be busy going and doing, to sit still for any amount of time. But here she did.

The flowers are still bright and flourishing thanks to the gardener who likely worked up until Vera was gone. If there are bodies here, we're going to have to tear it up. We're going to have to destroy the place that was always hers.

The one place no one else ever came.

The place she thought was safe.

In the small garden shed, Cole grabs two shovels, passing one to me. "I guess we should just"—he motions with the shovel, pretending to dig—"start anywhere?"

I swallow. Vera's presence in the house is undeniable, but if I really think about it, this is where I see her the most. Tearing up her garden will be the ultimate betrayal.

Then again, she's already betrayed me in the worst way possible. With that in mind, I stab the shovel into the ground. The dirt is hard and barely gives way, but I don't relent. I dig again, unearthing a bush of bright pink flowers.

Taking a cue from me, Cole walks to the opposite corner of the garden and begins to dig. He's faster than I am, and I swear his dirt must be looser than mine because he seems to clear a sizable space with relative ease, seven bushes of various flowers thrown aside in the time it takes me to remove two.

I pause, swiping the back of my hand across my forehead and huffing a breath.

"You good?"

At first I think he might be teasing me over how slow I'm going, but when I look up, there seems to be genuine concern in his eyes. I'm so confused by this man and who he is now. He's nothing like the boy I remember.

"I'm fine," I say, getting back to work.

Cole seems to be digging down deep, while I'm working to uproot the flowers across the surface, my arms burning from exertion.

"You can take a break," he says, when I've paused again.

"Didn't need your permission," I snap, out of breath.

He returns to work, then stops suddenly. "You know, sometimes I think you're nothing like her, but then...there she is."

My eyes narrow on him, his face painted with shadows. "Excuse me?"

"You claim to be so angry with Vera, you go on and on about the fact that she's cold and you could never under-stand her, but how are you any different? How have you ever been any different? You're her made over."

Rage grips my organs, forcing my throat to constrict. I grip the wood handle of the shovel. "You have no idea what you're talking about."

"Oh"—he chuckles to himself—"I do."

"I'm nothing like Vera. I have friends. Real friends." *Well, a friend, anyway.* "I'm a good person, Cole. Just because I'm not nice to you, because you've never been nice to me, doesn't mean anything."

"I'm being nice to you now," he points out. "All I've done is be nice to you since we arrived, Bridget. What more do you want from me?"

I open my mouth to argue, to give an example of when he hasn't been nice since my arrival home, but an example eludes me. Is he right?

"I've been nice to you since I came back to Bitter House. Yes, I was a shitty kid who was overcompensating for the fact that my house wasn't even mine, and you reminded me of that every chance you got, but I'm not that kid anymore. I guess you can't see that. To you, I'll always be the kid who teased and ignored you because I was jealous, but—"

"Jealous?" I cry out, nothing about that statement making sense. "Jealous of what? The fact that my parents were dead? The fact that my grandmother could hardly stand to look at me? That I was alone *all the time*?"

He swallows, dropping his gaze. "Perception versus reality, I guess." He meets my eyes again. "Because, from where I stood, I saw the big house, the fact that you got everything you could ever want—"

"Except love. A family."

"I had my mom, I won't apologize for that, but I had nothing else. Don't you see that? I'd lived in Bitter House since I was six years old. It was the only home I'd ever known, and yet I didn't have a room I could make my own. I didn't get to make requests for dinner or have birthday parties with all my friends. I walked on eggshells my entire life here. Add to that the fact that I didn't have the money to do half of what you did. I didn't have a car when I turned sixteen or a new phone when my screen cracked, like yours did all the time. And yeah, maybe looking back, those are pretty crappy things to complain about in the grand scheme of things, but when you were constantly being handed everything you could want and all of my things were shoved into the *one* room I was allowed to exist in inside this house I didn't belong in, it wasn't exactly the time of my life."

"So why fight to stay here, then?" I demand. "Why not just walk away?"

"Because it *is* mine now. It's proof that..." He stops, pressing his lips together with a huff, and looks away. "It's proof that Vera actually wanted me here. That I misread all of this. That she gave me the house over her own family because...maybe she thought of me as family, too. Maybe she...maybe she didn't hate me after all."

I stare at him, listening to his words, the truth of them in his voice, and I realize I've had him wrong all this time. We were just two kids living in this tomb of a house, feeling unwanted and out of place.

"I'm sorry," I say finally, my voice powerless. "I never thought of it like that."

He nods, returning to work.

"For the record, I don't think Vera was capable of hate. She didn't hate you. Mostly because she also couldn't love anyone, not since she lost her husband. There was something wrong with her. She was empty, I think. It wasn't us, it was her."

He doesn't look at me, but I can tell he's processing my words as his movements slow. "Well, like I said before, losing someone you love can do that to a person. It makes me sad for her more than anything."

I don't know what to say to that or how to feel, so I return to digging, but I quickly realize I have more to add.

"Also, for the record, I don't know how to get close to people anymore. The issue is still with me. Sometimes I don't even see that I'm being rude. I'm just...protecting myself. Vera really hurt me. And your mom, too. And you. The day I was sent away, it felt like my already small world just collapsed, and I'm scared to let anyone in, so I'm..." I smile to myself. "My friend calls me a cactus. I'm prickly, but it's just because I've been hurt by everyone I've ever trusted, you included. It's self-preservation at its finest."

He cocks his head to the side. "I was a kid, B."

"You were twenty."

"It wasn't my house. Or my mom's for that matter. It devastated her to make you leave, but she had a job to do. It was never because she didn't care about you. Or that I didn't either, for that matter. Because I did. I *do*. As much as I teased you, as much as I picked on you, you were always family. You have to know that."

"Family?" I ask softly. "Is that why you punched Cory Steele in school after he made fun of me?"

He jerks his head backward with surprise. "You knew about that?"

"The whole school knew about that," I say with a scoff.

"You never asked me about it back then."

I shrug. "I'm asking now."

"Cory was an asshole." His response is clipped.

"Was it over me?" I push again.

He sighs. "Look, a lot of people talked shit about you back then, but not around me. Cory knew that, and he chose to do it anyway. There were consequences."

A strange sort of warmth blooms in my chest. "You were the only one allowed to pick on me, hmm?"

He meets my eyes briefly with one corner of his mouth upturned. "Something like that."

"Well, thank you."

"Don't mention it." He waves me off. "But we should really get back to work before it gets too dark to see anything."

We're already almost at that point, so he's right. We work in silence for another hour, finding nothing. The entire garden has been destroyed, including the earth around Vera's bench, though it's cemented into the ground and can't be moved.

"There's nothing," Cole says, out of breath. His entire T-shirt is soaked through with dark patches of sweat. He stabs his shovel into the ground, leaving it standing on its own. "Nothing here. This was a waste of time."

I stare around at the mess we've made. "Maybe we have to dig deeper."

"How much deeper can we go?" He looks around from the hole where he's standing, the dirt reaching just level with the top of his head. "I'm nearly six foot tall. You really think Vera could've dug a hole like this by herself?"

I smile to myself. "If Vera had enough time, I'm not sure there's anything she couldn't have done."

"Fair enough." He tries to pull himself up out of the dirt, clawing at the ground to find a place to get hold, and when I stick out my hand to help him up, he hesitates before taking hold of it, the two of us dragging him out of the hole and to his feet. Once he's standing, I realize he hasn't released my hand. We're so close I can smell the scent of him —an intense mixture of sweat and earth and cologne. We look down at the place where we're connected, his hand in mine, and all at once, we drop hands and take a step back.

He rubs a hand over the back of his neck, smearing mud wherever he touches. "We can dig some more tomorrow, if you'd like, but it's getting dark. We should...we should get inside and clean up."

I nod. As much as I want to argue, to insist we stay and keep digging until we find something, I know he's right. It's too dark to properly see anything at this point.

We put our shovels away for now and make our way into the house. There is dirt under my fingernails and in my hair, and once I'm in the shower, I watch the mud painting the water brown as it washes down the drain.

I feel strangely empty, though I don't know why. Not finding anything in the garden should be a good thing. It's not like I wanted to prove that Vera was a murderer. But it leaves me with more questions than answers. Who is writing the letters? Why did they lie? What do they want from us?

Though I know we can go out and dig more tomorrow, I think Cole is probably right. We made quite a dent in the garden and the earth beneath it, and there was nothing suspicious at all.

Which makes it clear that whoever is writing the letters thought we wouldn't check. Maybe they thought we'd take their word for it. Or maybe they thought their warning not to leave would play some sort of reverse psychology trick on us, and we'd head for the hills without looking back.

I suspect the letter writer could be Zach or Jenn—or maybe the two of them working together—but I'm more determined than ever to find out for sure. When I get out of the shower, I log in to my banking app and check my balance. There's not much in there now that my half of the rent has come out, but there's enough. I open my browser and search for a security camera with decent reviews that will get here by tomorrow. When I find one, I add it to my cart and, without allowing myself to second-guess the unplanned expenditure, I place the order.

Vera was always old-fashioned about security. She believed the gate was enough, but I need to know who's leaving the letters, and as soon as the camera arrives, I'll be able to do just that.

Downstairs, I find Cole in the sitting room with a glass of some amber-colored liquid on the rocks.

He looks up, clearly surprised to see me. "I thought you'd gone to bed."

"Not yet." Though my body is tired and sore enough I know the second I hit the mattress, I'm done for. "Thought I'd come down for a drink instead."

He stands up. "Can I make you something?"

"Vodka soda's perfect," I tell him. "Extra—"

"Extra lime," he says at the same time, nodding. "I remember your preference for all things sour."

I sink down onto the couch on the opposite end of where he'd been sitting, curling a leg up under me. My hair is still wet, slight waves forming around my face, and I tuck both sides behind my ears as he makes his way across the room from the copper bar cart to hand me my glass.

I take a sip, the burn of the drink already soothing me somewhere deep in my core. "You know, I used to be so jealous of Vera and Edna when I'd find them in this room at night. They were always so...otherworldly, I guess. They'd be having *important adult conversations,* always in hushed voices, drinks in their hands. I remember thinking, 'I want to be just like them someday.' Important, you know? Powerful. Back then, I thought Vera was the epitome of power."

He takes a sip of his own drink, nodding before crunching on a piece of ice. "They always seemed to have it all together. That's what I remember. I don't know if I ever saw Vera lose her cool or even seem stressed. She was just... stone."

"That's a good way to describe her, actually. Stone. Unbreakable." My voice cracks, and I feel betraying tears fill my eyes.

He looks at me but doesn't ask what's wrong. I don't think he needs to. Instead, he just stares, waiting for me to speak.

"I just can't believe she's actually gone, can you? I'm sorry. I don't know why I'm crying. I hadn't spoken to her in over a decade, but I guess I always thought a day would come where we'd fix it, you know? That she'd tell me what I did wrong, and I could make it right somehow. And now..." I sniffle, drying my eyes, then force a laugh. "Wow, I'm so sorry. I'm exhausted, can you tell?"

He doesn't laugh, just stares at me with those pitying eyes that I love to hate. "You lost your grandmother, Bridget. It's normal to be sad, no matter how complicated the relationship was. But, for what it's worth, I hope you know you aren't to blame. There was nothing you needed to fix. No matter what, there is nothing you could've done that would justify Vera making you leave. That's not how family is supposed to work."

I stare at him for a long time. There's something in the timbre of his voice that makes me think he's speaking from experience. "Do you...I mean, are your grandparents still alive? I've never heard you talk about them."

"No," he says, taking another sip of his drink. "Not the ones that matter, anyway. I never knew my dad's parents, and Edna's dad died before I was born. Her mom, the grandma I knew, passed away when I was twelve."

Right around the time I moved in. He was going through so much, and I never saw it. "I'm sorry."

He runs his teeth over his bottom lip. "Happens to the best of us."

"How different do you think life would've been if we'd gotten along back then?"

He looks over at me. "Us?" His hand waves back and forth between our chests.

"Yeah. I mean, you were two years older than me. We could've been more like siblings."

"I think, in general, siblings fight too," he says simply.

"But they also love each other."

"I fought someone for you. You wouldn't call that love?"

His words shock me. "What?"

He swirls his drink, downing the last of it and moving to the bar cart to refill it. "Maybe in our own strange way, we showed love how we could. Just like you were jealous of Catherine Marshall." When he looks back at me, the grin on his face is positively devilish. "Although, if we'd been siblings, I'm pretty sure *that* sort of jealousy would've been illegal or, at the very least, frowned upon."

My face burns, ears ringing. "I was not jealous of Catherine. She was just...awful." I think of the many days I passed Catherine and Cole walking out of his bedroom, her hair mussed, lips red. I picture the way she'd sneer at me, how she told everyone at school that I was basically my grandmother's servant, though it was the furthest thing from the truth.

Vera was far too busy ignoring me to ever ask me to do anything.

"If you say so," he teases, sitting down on the couch again and leaning backward, one foot on the marble coffee table.

"I'm serious. I didn't like her being here."

"Or any of the other girls I brought home." One of his dark brown brows quirks, and I have the sudden urge to lunge forward and press it right back down.

"She was cruel. She started rumors about me. Teased me."

His eyes narrow, jaw dropping, and I can practically see the gears turning as he processes what I've told him. "Wait. Are you serious?"

I press my lips together, giving him a look that says I'm not in the mood to play. "Come on, you knew she did."

"I didn't. I swear I didn't. I never would've..." He looks down. "I punched Cory over talking shit about you. Do you really think I would've brought her here—that I would've been dating her at all—if I'd known she was doing the same?"

The seriousness in his voice startles me. Could he really not have known that was happening back then? "Whatever. It doesn't matter anymore. It was a long time ago. I just thought you were obnoxious with all the girls you brought home. Security was important to Vera. We didn't need to have strangers in the house."

"Oh, come on. Vera told me herself that it was fine for me to have people over, otherwise I would've never done it.

Mom wouldn't have let me and you know it." He leans back farther with a cocky grin that makes my blood boil. "Besides, they weren't strangers. I'd say I knew them *pretty well.*"

"Yeah, well, you knew most of the girls at our school *pretty well.*"

He grins at me. "Sure, but not the cactus across the hall."

"I never should have told you that." I cover my eyes with one hand.

"Too late now."

Looking back up at him, I narrow my gaze. "I wasn't jealous. I just happened to think you chose your girlfriends horribly."

He turns on the couch until he's facing me, one leg tucked up under him, mirroring my position. If either of us move an inch forward, our knees will be touching.

"Okay, one, most of them weren't my girlfriends. And two, who would you rather me date? Someone like you?"

"Would that have been so bad? Someone who actually cared about you? Who cared about something other than sleeping with you, I mean? You were cycling through girls back then so fast, and no one cared. Would someone like me have really been so boring?"

He snorts, but there's nothing cruel in his eyes or tone. We're having fun now. "Someone so prim and proper she probably hadn't been kissed yet? We both know you wouldn't have known how to handle me at that age. But, for the record, I wasn't using those girls back then, and they weren't using me. We both got what we wanted, simple as that."

"Meaningless sex."

"Among other things."

"Like?"

"Distraction. Attention. Probably the same reason you were dating whatever guy you were dating around that time."

"I wasn't dating anyone. Like you just said, I was a prim and proper girl who'd never been kissed, remember?"

Something dark flashes in his eyes. "When did that change?"

"When did I stop being prim and proper?" I laugh.

"When did you have your first kiss?"

My cheeks are suddenly an inferno as shock sweeps through me. I hum, staring up at the ceiling to hide it. "Sam Kellerman. I was"—I think back—"seventeen. He kissed me at prom."

His face is stoic as he nods and takes another drink. "And? How was it?"

"Uneventful," I admit. "Though not at the time."

He chuckles.

"And you? When did you have your first kiss? The ripe old age of ten?"

There's that lopsided grin again. "Twelve. And then sex at fourteen."

My heart picks up speed. "That's so young."

He shrugs. "Probably, but it didn't feel like it at the time. I'm not, like, traumatized over it or anything. It was with a girl I liked well enough. Didn't work out, which was fine, and then, once I got the hang of things, I figured I may as well have fun."

None of what he's saying truly surprises me. Cole was twelve when we met, and I watched all throughout his teenage years while he dated and hooked up with several girls, many of whom I didn't know since he'd met them through his job or friends, and they went to different schools, but none of whom ever seemed very nice.

"Are you still that way?" I ask, posing the question I'm dying to have an answer to as simple curiosity. "Wild and free? Or have you settled down some?"

His smile is soft, distant. Clearly, he's thinking hard about something. "I'm not the kid I was, no. I've grown up, but I'm no saint if that's what you mean. I like to think I choose women that I'm a better match for now."

"Well, you must be pretty different, since you haven't had a single girl over, and it's been all of, what, three days? The old you would've been going stir crazy."

He sucks his drink down. "You're awfully interested in my sex life, B."

"Just trying to decide if—I mean, if this thing is going to be long term—we should come up with some sort of system. Like a sock on the door sort of thing. I'd hate to walk in on something I may never recover from."

"Same here." He eyes me. "Do I need to worry about that?"

"Do I?"

His lips twist together, his gaze positively searing. "How about I let you know?"

"Same."

He nods, then stands, rubbing his hand over his thigh. "I should get to bed. I'll see you in the morning, Cactus."

Once I realize what he's said, I turn to tell him to stop calling me that, but he's already gone. I feel his absence in every part of my body.

What the hell is happening here, and why do I not want it to stop?

CHAPTER FOURTEEN

VERA BITTER

When I met Reggie, I was still bitter. Still grieving the loss of Harold—though I don't think that will ever stop. I was a relatively young woman, with two daughters away at college and a house much too big for me. Despite its enormity and —some might say—*impracticality*, I know Harold always wanted me to keep Bitter House if anything happened to him, and I have absolutely no intention of ever leaving, much to his family's chagrin. The house had belonged to the Bitter family for generations, and with him gone, I have no doubt his brother is seething at the thought of us here, but this is my home, my children's home, and this is where we will stay.

Reggie came along when I was still trying to find my place. I've always been a stubborn child. Momma and Daddy used to say I'll be too stubborn to die one day, and I have no evidence to the contrary.

As a girl, I spent many a night dreaming of things girls

back then had no business dreaming about. A career. A life. A legacy. I never dreamed of men. Or women, for that matter. I dreamed of myself. Of changing the world, making a name for myself.

Of course, eventually, you start to realize the world has other ideas about what women should be doing with their lives. Meeting Harold gave me a reason to put all of that aside. To set my dreams down with love and hope that someday I could return to them.

When I met Reggie, I swear I felt all of my dreams shrivel and die. Not at first, no. He was much too smart for that. Aren't they all? At first, he was everything I needed. He was loving. Attentive. He made me laugh. Made me feel—if not completely whole, at least the closest I'd been since Harold's passing. Stupidly, I believed he could fix me. He could make me feel the things I'd resigned myself to never feeling again.

I thought he could love the girls as much as Harold had. That he could be there for them the way a girl needs her father, walk them down the aisle in his place, dance with them at their wedding. I thought by marrying him I was not only healing my heart, but healing our family.

No one could ever replace Harold, but to have someone who wanted to step into his space in our lives was such a relief when my heart desperately needed respite. It was a balm, not a fix, but I believed I could learn to love him like I needed to.

We had a quick courtship and were married six months after we met. That should've been my first sign of trouble, that he was too good to be true, but my mind was such a mess back then I just didn't see it.

He was, and shall remain, my biggest mistake.

It only took two days after the wedding for him to hit me for the first time. And I noticed the way his eyes lingered on my girls when they were home from college, the way he'd watch them in the pool with their friends.

I may have been blinded by my pain, but I wasn't stupid. I was stubborn and, I've learned, that can be a superpower.

CHAPTER FIFTEEN

BRIDGET

The next morning, Cole is working from the dining room table, so I make my way to the living room to give him some space. Though I know my package hasn't arrived yet, I check the front door just in case, and I find the next letter there waiting for me.

I bend down, picking it up and turning it over in my hand. This is letter number three of the promised six, and so far, we have no more answers, just a ton more questions. I'm not sure I have the stomach for whatever this may hold.

Still, my curiosity gets the best of me, and I tear it open as I cross the porch and lean against the railing, scanning the yard and road in the distance, wondering if the mysterious sender of these letters might be out there somewhere, watching me, waiting to see how I'll react.

With that in mind, I turn my back toward the gate and pull out the letter, unfolding it quickly. A lump forms in my throat at the familiar font.

. . .

Bridget,

By now, you've discovered one of Vera's darkest secrets, and you understand what a dangerous woman she was. I can't blame you if you want to leave or call the police, but thank you for not doing so. I won't stop you from doing whatever you decide is for the best once everything has come out, but there is still so much you need to know and that can only happen if you wait for the remaining letters.

I'm so sorry to say the next secret will be the most painful, but it is necessary, Bridget. You have to know everything, and unfortunately, I'm tasked with the burden of telling you.

Of all the blood on Vera Bitter's hands, the worst is that of her daughter and son-in-law.

Vera Bitter killed your parents.

Their accident was never an accident.

It's the reason she cut all remaining ties with your family. It's the reason she was alone in the end.

I'm so sorry, but it's true.

I only wish it wasn't.

Signed,
A friend

CHAPTER SIXTEEN

BRIDGET

I drop to my knees in a second, my legs suddenly losing all feeling.

Vera Bitter killed your parents.

Vera Bitter killed your parents.

Vera Bitter killed your parents.

Vera Bitter killed your parents.

Vera. Bitter. Killed. Your. Parents.

The words echo in my head, my temples throbbing. It's not possible. It's not...no. No.

No. No. No. No. No.

Vera wouldn't. Vera didn't.

She couldn't.

They're lying. This person, this letter writer, is lying. Just like they lied about the bodies in the garden. Like they've lied about everything.

Snap out of it, Bridget.

Vera didn't have secrets. She was a sad, lonely old woman who had given up on everything and everyone. Who pushed people away so she wouldn't get hurt again. Who closed herself off to the world. That's it.

This is clearly an attempt to make me question everything, make me scared, make me leave.

I can't catch my breath. Tears prick my eyes as I try to reason with myself, try to calm myself down. *It's okay. You're okay.*

They're lying.

They have to be lying.

She loved Mom. I watched her cry at the funeral. I saw with my own eyes the way she buckled in on herself, the way Edna had to hold her up and how Uncle Marcus had helped carry her away from the cemetery. No one could fake that. No one could make their eyes that empty.

But...if anyone could, it would be Vera. It's like I said last night, if Vera wanted to do something, she'd find a way.

I'm still out of it, my chest constricting with fear and confusion, when I notice the man walking toward me. It takes several seconds for my brain to begin working again and piece together what's happening.

The brown socks.

Dark blue jeans.

Green shirt.

Dark eyes.

Dark hair.

He's staring at me, down on his knees so we're eye level. He's saying something, but I can't hear him. I'm underwater. The paper in my hands is gone, and I see him staring down at it. My knees are warm, and I feel him take hold of me, feel myself being lifted from under my arms. When I look down, there's a smear of blood on the wooden porch. My knee must've been sliced open when I landed.

Weirdly, I can't even feel it.

"Bridget!" His shout brings me back to reality, and I get the feeling it's not the first time he's screamed at me.

I blink, tears cascading down my cheeks, and open my mouth. He's holding my face in both hands and somehow, we're in the kitchen. I'm sitting on the edge of the table, and he's in front of me, pleading with me.

"It can't be true..." I whisper. A hand goes to my chest, clutching my heart as I try to focus.

He's bending down in front of me now, pulling up the leg of my pajama pants. "You're bleeding," he says softly, standing back up to meet my eyes again. "I'm going to get something to clean you up. I'll be right back, okay?"

I'm nearly positive I've nodded, but he stands there anyway, watching me closely. "Okay?" he repeats.

"Yes."

With that, he disappears from the room but returns in what feels like mere seconds. Or hours. I can't make my heart—my eyes, my head—focus, my thoughts swirling with the revelations, and the entire room seems to be spinning.

It hurts.

It all just hurts.

I'm so sick of the way it hurts.

He bends down again, rubbing my knee with a wet piece

of gauze. It stings slightly, but I can hardly feel it. Every part of my body is numb except for the inside, which hurts enough for all of it.

He's pressing a bandage on my knee when my eyes finally find their focus. When he stands, he tucks my hair behind my ears on either side. His eyes search mine like he's looking for the answers to a quiz he's about to take. "Are you okay?"

"How could I be?" I choke out. It's the only thing I can manage to say.

His face cracks, wrinkles forming, and he leans his head to the side. "B, you know it isn't true. Vera would've never hurt your mom. She loved her. No matter your opinions of her, you have to believe—you have to *know*—she loved her. Besides, the accident was just that: an accident. You were in the car. You know that no one caused it. Vera couldn't have done it. It's impossible."

He grabs the letter from where it rests next to me on the table and folds it in half, tucking it into the back pocket of his jeans. "I'm not sure what this person is doing. I don't know what their endgame is here, but we've already proven that they're liars. There were no bodies in the flower garden, and aside from the gun in the closet—which Mom already explained—it's nothing. They've proven nothing, done nothing other than to scare and upset us, which is clearly what they want. I say you just stop opening the letters. Forget about them. Someone just wants to shake you up or scare you off, and you can't let them. *I* won't let them."

"I can't stop. I have to know. I have to, Cole." I can tell

from the way he's looking at me, he doesn't understand. I'm not even sure I understand myself. "I know it would be easier to just stop reading them, but what if they are telling the truth? We need to know. I ordered a camera," I add. "So we'll see who's leaving them. It should be here later today."

"Okay, great." He nods, petting the side of my head. "Great. So that will give us peace of mind, at least. We'll figure out who's doing this—my money is on Zach—and then we can move on. I talked to Mom earlier, and she said Jenn and Zach have already hired an attorney to fight us over the house, but her attorney assured her there's nothing to worry about. The will is legal. On top of that, apparently Vera put some sort of clause in there that states if anyone contests it and loses, they lose whatever they were entitled to in the will in the first place, which means Jenn and Zach would be stupid to try. Our attorney doesn't seem to think they will."

I nod. I hadn't really thought about Aunt Jenn actually trying to fight us over this, though it makes sense that she would. I understand where she's coming from, but I'm not sure that the house is worth what she was given as an inheritance, assuming she, Zach, and Jonah received all of Vera's estate. She could buy a dozen houses just like this one if she wanted and still have plenty left over.

Suddenly, something deep within my mind ignites. "Wait." I put a hand on his arm, brought all the way back to the present by something he just said. "The flower garden."

He gives me a dubious look. "Huh?"

"You said we didn't find anything in the flower garden,

and you were right." I jump down off the table, ignoring the pain in my knee. "Oh my god!"

"Are we just stating facts now, or do you want to elaborate?" he asks, chasing after me as I dart through the house and upstairs. My leg hurts worse now, my feeling coming back, but it's easy to drown it out when I've found the missing puzzle piece.

Upstairs, I shut my door and lock it before he reaches me, quickly changing into my clothes and shoes for the day.

"Are you going to tell me what's going on?" he calls through the door. "Should I be worried? Did you hit your head?"

A few moments later, I swing the door back open, standing in front of him in jeans, a T-shirt, and my sneakers. With a deep breath in, I say, "We were looking in the wrong place."

Then, I zip past him again, and he chases me back down the stairs and rushes to slip on his shoes by the door before following me out of the house.

"The wrong place? What does that even mean? The wrong place?" he calls, out of breath as he tries to keep up with me.

"We checked the flower garden."

"Right. Like the letter said."

I spin around, shaking my head and biting back a growing grin on my lips because I'm almost positive I've figured it out. What we missed. It was right in front of our faces the whole time, and I overlooked it. "No. The letter said *garden*, not *flower* garden."

He narrows his eyes, staring up toward the sky. "What? I didn't realize there was another option."

I point toward the woods. "Just before you reach the woods over there, there used to be a vegetable garden. I remember seeing pictures in the photo albums in Vera's room of my mom and Aunt Jenn picking vegetables with the gardener. I asked her about it before, and she told me at one point, she and my grandfather had all of their vegetables grown on their land. When he died, she let the garden go with him. I don't know why I didn't think of it until now. That has to be what the letter was talking about, and we just assumed they meant the flower garden."

I spin back around, hurrying forward to the shed to grab our shovels. I pass his to him and then head toward the patch of land where I'm sure the old garden used to be based on the pictures I saw.

"Okay, but the garden is gone now," Cole says. "So for someone to have known about it, it would have to be someone who was around back then. An old employee. Or your aunt or cousins."

I nod, setting to work. "Or someone else who saw the pictures I did. It was here. Come on, help me dig." My hands burn with fresh blisters from yesterday's digging, which only makes this all so much harder. Each stab of the shovel into the ground is a tear to the soft flesh of my palms, a white-hot scorching of blistered, raw skin.

He looks unsure, and I realize only then that he's still dressed in nice clothes for his work calls, and the shoes he slipped on moments ago are clearly not meant for hard labor.

Stopping to blow air on my burning palms, I say, "You don't have to if you don't want to. Or if you're busy. I'll let you know if I find anything."

He pulls his lips into his mouth, looking away, but eventually he sighs and joins me on my hunt.

The ground is softer here, or maybe I'm just less tired or more determined, but the whole process seems to move faster despite the pain I'm in. Fewer roots, perhaps. Eventually, we each have waist-deep holes dug and are working on expanding them, moving toward each other. My entire body seems to ache, as if I've been run over by a truck, muscles sore and bruised from the work I'm putting in.

When Cole stabs his shovel in the ground, and we're met with a dull thud, we freeze. My palms scream from the sudden relief. He looks up at me, a cautious smile on his full lips.

"Do you see something?" I ask, my body going icy.

He swallows, his dark eyes filled with terror as his gaze falls down. Then, he bends. I scramble out of the hole I've dug and make my way over to him, watching as he uses his hands to carefully unearth something there.

Soon, it's clear what it is that we're staring at, and it's as if my entire body has been plunged into icy water.

"It's a hand," I say, my eyes trailing over the white bones of the fingers he's uncovered.

He grabs fistfuls of mud, throwing them back. He plucks a worm from between his fingers, tossing it aside before he pulls the final bit of dirt back. His shoulders go tense. "It's a body," he says softly as the bone of the arm comes into view. His eyes find mine again. "Whoever wrote that letter, they were telling the truth."

Which means they could be telling the truth about all of the rest of it, too.

CHAPTER SEVENTEEN

BRIDGET

Cole slips out of the hole in the earth, dusting off his hands on the butt of his jeans. He's out of breath from fear and exertion as he stares down into the hole. All we can see at the moment is the arm. Cole stopped digging once we had it uncovered, but I'm positive the rest of the skeleton is there. And, since the note said *bodies*, I'm assuming there could be more than one.

"We need to call the police," he says firmly, turning his head to look at me.

I nod. "I know." My chest feels empty and cold, stretched out like a deflated balloon. All of this anticipation and determination, and now, I'm not sure why I was so determined to find something. There is no sense of accomplishment that comes with this discovery, only devastation and fear.

"They'll be able to dig the rest of the body up, to tell

who it is. They'll be able to find more if there's more to find."

I take in a deep breath. "Um." Swallow. "How will we... I mean, how will we tell the police we found it? How will we say we knew where to look?" I can't bear to meet his eyes. Though I knew nothing about this body before today, somehow this feels like my fault. My family, my problem. It feels like I've dragged him into it.

"We'll show them the letters. They may even be able to figure out who's sending them."

Again, I nod, but it doesn't feel like me. It feels like someone else is controlling me. Like I'm a puppet on a string. "Right."

"We should go to the house and call," he says, taking a step back. "If we dig any more, they could say we tampered with the crime scene or something."

"Okay." But instead of following him, instead of walking in the direction he's heading, though I know he's right, I walk toward the dirt pile. I grab my shovel and begin pushing the dirt into the hole with all my strength, covering up everything we've just discovered.

"Wait. What are you doing?" He runs forward, grabbing my arms to stop me, but I shove him off.

"*Stop! Let me go!*" I cry, working harder. Faster. I watch as the snow-white bones disappear beneath the dark soil, as the darkness swallows them whole.

He reaches for the shovel again, trying to stop me. He grabs hold of the shovel, and try as I might to pull it away from him, I can't get it out of his hand. We're at an impasse, both of us holding the shovel's handle with an iron grip. "What are you thinking, B? Talk to me. Tell me why, and I'll help you. But I need to understand what's happening."

I stop at the calm in his tone, staring up at him. I was so worried he'd force me to stop, so worried he wouldn't listen to me, but it seems he's prepared to. Perhaps he won't agree, but at least I can try. My arms burn from exertion, aching like bruises as I turn, releasing the shovel to him.

"I...look, I know it doesn't make any sense when I'm the one who forced you to help me look for the body, but I don't want to call the police yet," I say.

He locks his jaw, looking toward the ground then back to me. When he speaks again, somehow his voice is even gentler. "We...we found a body. We have to report it. We can't just pretend it didn't happen."

"I know." I put my hands up, pleading my case as I try to make my sudden change of heart make sense to both of us simultaneously. "I know. And we will call the police and tell them everything. I promise you we will. I just...there are three more letters."

"Bridget, this is a body. An actual human skeleton. Letters or no letters, we can't just sit on this information. We could be charged with covering up a crime or something." He's pleading with me to understand, and I do, but I can't give up. I have to know the rest.

"I swear to you, we will call the police as soon as we've gotten the last letter. It's just three more letters, three more days. What if the last ones are the most important? What if there are bigger, more terrible secrets than this? I mean, if they've already told us about the body and my parents, what else could there be? What if it only gets worse from here? If we call the police now, there's a chance we might never know what else is out there. If we'd found the body last night and called the police...I might not know the truth about my parents." My voice cracks, and his face goes soft, suddenly understanding.

"We still don't know that what they said is the truth. We have no proof Vera was involved in your parents' accident. It doesn't make sense to me that she could've been. The police never said there was anything suspicious about it."

My chest tightens, and I stare at him, wanting to say more, to beg him to side with me, but I don't know if there's a point. If he wants to call the police, I'll have to let him and that kills me.

"You really want to wait for the last three letters?"

His words surprise me, filling me with hope as I clutch my hands together in front of my chest. "Three more days," I tell him. "And then we can tell the police everything. Hand over the letters. We can say it took us that long to find the body. We'll cover it all back up for now, just in case anyone were to come snooping, and then in three days, we'll report this. I promise." I stare down into the hole. "That body has been there a long time, Cole. Three more days won't hurt anything. Vera is dead and gone. We aren't saving anyone by turning her in now."

He looks away, clearly wrestling with what he wants to say. "If she did this, if she hurt someone—killed someone—

we can't protect her. Promise me you understand that. I won't keep this secret forever. It's too heavy."

I touch his arm lightly. "No. I won't protect her. I promise that's not what this is about. I owe her nothing. I just want to know everything. That's it."

With a tight jaw, he nods, then hands me the shovel back. "Let's get to work, then."

We work together to push the dirt back into the ground —much easier than digging in the first place—and pat it down. Cole jumps on top of it, his shoes covered in mud, until the ground is nearly as flat as when we found it, though it's obviously been recently dug up, the patches of grass intermingling with patches of dirt.

"We should get inside and clean up," he says, holding out his hand for mine.

Without thinking, I slip it into his palm. Both our hands are dry and caked with dirt, but somehow, it doesn't bother me. We're in this together in every way that counts.

Cole stares down at our hands, his body stiff. It's only then that I realize he'd been waiting for me to hand him my shovel, not take his hand.

A wave of ice crashes over me as I pull my hand away, replacing it with the shovel in his. "Sorry about that. I'm just...tired."

"Yeah. Don't worry about it." He turns, directing us back to the house. With a hint of a smile, he adds, "There are worse things you could've put in my hand."

"For example?" My face is the temperature of the sun,

scalding and melting off my bones. *What the hell was I thinking?*

He hums, thinking. "Mayonnaise, for one."

"You don't like mayonnaise?"

He laughs. "Not in my hand."

I'm grateful for the way he's eased the tension, even if my face is still burning.

"Also, a live rat."

"Dead one's okay, though?" I quip.

"I'd prefer no rats be put into my hands, thanks."

"Noted."

He bumps my arm with his, and his smile warms me to my core. I hope I'm telling him *thank you* without words as I stare at him, so appreciative of what he's doing.

We put the shovels away, and when we reach the front yard, we stop in our tracks at the sight waiting for us. I squint my eyes in the sun, trying to make sense of it. Three women are making their way up the drive.

It clicks for me all at once when I realize who they are. I'd nearly forgotten about the neighbors.

Once their faces come into clearer view, I recognize them from their visit a few days ago. I haven't returned their casserole dishes or thanked them for being so kind, but still, my body bristles at their intrusion. Something about the women bothers me, but I can't put my finger on what it is.

And if you look up 'bad timing' online, I'm convinced you'd find a photo of us at this moment. The two of us, caked in dirt, looking guilty as sin, with a literal skeleton in our backyard.

Jane waves at us with a hand over her head. "Well, hello there." She's wearing a black skirt and plain white T-shirt, looking positively sleek.

The woman behind her, Lily, has on a paisley dress, her wild gray hair blowing in every direction. "You've got a little mud on you"—she pats the air in the direction of our heads down to our toes—"er, well, sort of everywhere."

"Everything alright?" Jane asks when they get closer, her blue eyes studying us carefully, taking in our ragged appearances.

"Yeah," I say, thinking quickly. "We're redoing the flower garden. Most of the plants were dying, and I know how much Vera loved that space, so we've been working on revamping it."

Jane's eyes dart toward the backyard, though she can't see anything from here. "Yes, she did love that garden. I'm surprised to hear everything died. It was so pretty the last time we were out there."

"Make sure you plant some zinnias and snapdragons," Cate adds. "Those were her favorite. Oh, and dahlias."

"And hydrangeas," Lily says. "Foxglove, oleander, and azaleas."

"We'll make you a list," Jane tells me. "We've got plenty at our houses too, so we're happy to help you get started with a few cuttings and seeds."

"Thank you." I scratch near my eye, where a speck of mud seems to be drying my skin out. "We'd appreciate that. It's all pretty new to us."

Jane clasps her hands in front of her chest. "Well, we just wanted to come by and see how you two were holding up. Have you gotten to try any of the casseroles we brought over?"

"One of them," I tell her. "And we'll probably have the other tonight, actually. Thank you again for bringing them. I'll be sure to return your dishes and bag once I've washed everything."

She waves off the suggestion. "Trust me, I have plenty where those came from. There's no rush. Is there anything we can do for you? Some cleaning maybe? Or distraction? We're going to see a play in town later and would love for you to join us."

"Oh, um," I say, wincing. "We really appreciate the offer, but I have work to catch up on, and we're still trying to do things little by little around here. It's so kind of you, though."

"Once we get the house all set up to our liking, we'll have you lovely ladies over for dinner," Cole says, his voice dripping with charm. "How does that sound?"

"You trying to poison us, Cole Warner?" Cate asks, flashing him a wide grin.

"You know I'd never."

"We'll let you take the first bite," Lily says skeptically.

I'm starting to warm up to her.

Jane sighs. "Okay, well, we don't want to be a bother, but let's not be strangers, alright? Vera was a very good friend to us, and I know it would be important to her that we take good care of you." Her eyes linger on me. "We're just down the street if you need anything, and our phone numbers are on the fridge."

"Cole has them, too," Cate says.

"Right," Jane agrees. "So, if you need anything, know our door is open. Day or night."

"Most of us don't sleep well anyway," Lily says. "Unless there's a full moon." She winks.

"We really—" Before I can finish my sentence, we're interrupted by the sound of the gate opening at the end of the driveway and a black Mercedes pulling up toward the house.

My shoulders tense at the sight of Zach stepping out of his car, his perfectly coiffed head of shiny, blond hair coming into view before his face.

"Friend of yours?" Lily asks under her breath.

"No," Cole says.

"He's Vera's grandson and a realtor. He wants us to sell the house," I say at the same time.

"You're not going to do it, are you?" Jane asks, clearly horrified.

"No," I tell her. "I don't plan on selling the house any time soon."

"Greetings, cousin," Zach calls, his voice uncomfortably formal as he stalks across the yard. He pulls his sunglasses up from his eyes, surveying us carefully. "Been playing in the mud, have we?"

"Zach," I mutter. "Edna told us you're not having much luck with your lawyer trying to steal the house from us."

"More like take back what's rightfully ours," he says.

Dropping his dark glasses back over his eyes, he digs into his pocket and pulls out his phone. "Since the legal way is going to be such a headache, Mom and I want to make you an offer on the place. Three times more than it's worth based on my already generous comps. What do you say?" He turns the phone around so I can see the number Aunt Jenn has texted him. It's likely not a quarter of what Vera left them, but it's still a ridiculous amount of money.

Every eye in the vicinity is on me, though this decision isn't solely mine. To my surprise, when I look at Cole, he's waiting to hear my answer too.

I don't have to think about it. "I've already told you I don't want to sell this place." More so now than ever before, I'm positive about that. Even if I wasn't furious with how Zach and Aunt Jenn are handling this, we can't let them find what's in the backyard until we decide what to do about it. "That hasn't changed."

His brows pinch together. "You're being ridiculous. Don't let your stubbornness cause you to make a stupid decision. You need the money. We both know you do. Vera didn't leave you a dime. Let us help you. It's what family does."

The word *family* stings like a slap to the face. Zach isn't foolish. I'm the little girl who didn't have a family, and he thinks he can use that against me now, prod at my bruises until I give in, but it won't work.

"You heard the girl," Lily says, moving to step in front of me. Her voice has taken on the tone of a mother who's at her wit's end. She juts her chin up. "Go on now. Vera left the house to Bridget for a reason. It's hers. She wouldn't want it sold to someone else—*any*one else. This house meant too much to her."

"Look, lady, I have no idea who you are, but this is between me and Bridget—"

"And she's already given an answer." Lily is a full head shorter than Zach, but from the way she's looking at him, you'd never know it. She's formidable. It's the only way I know to describe her. She's the type of woman you could easily trick young children into believing is a witch, both because of the wild, wiry gray hair framing her face and because she is clearly the type of person to get things done.

I see why Vera must've liked her.

"We won't make this generous of an offer again," Zach says, still staring at Lily, though he's clearly talking to me.

"Would you look at that, ladies?" She pulls back with a wry grin, winking at Jane. "Here I thought we were the old ones, but this little peacock is clearly hard of hearing."

"She said she's not interested. She's staying. So you should be leaving," Jane says, her voice stony. She's equally terrifying, and I can practically picture her pouncing on him, thumping him on the head. I can't explain it, but she just has that look about her. The mental image nearly makes me smile. "Now."

Cate moves to stand next to her so the three of them form a wall in front of us, and my heart swells.

Zach looks around them, peering at me, and shakes his head. "Don't let your pride screw you, Bridget. You can't even afford to keep this house from caving in, and we all know it. This money could change your life."

Lily moves into his line of sight and plasters a sugar-sweet smile on her rosy lips. "I don't think you're hearing me. If you say another word to her, I'm going to call the police."

"Already on it," Cate says, pulling a phone out of the pocket of her yoga pants.

"Go, Zach," I say. "Leave. I'm not interested, and I won't change my mind."

He scoffs, swatting a hand in our direction as he walks away and back to his car, his shoulders swaying, head held high. Now I understand why Jane called him a peacock.

As he disappears back down the drive, the women turn back to look at us.

"Thank you," I say softly. "Really. I hate that you had to see that."

"Don't be ridiculous. We've been around a long time, honey. We've all seen much worse than him. This house meant everything to Vera, Bridget. You know that." Lily's eyes are so serious, it's painful. "Promise me you won't give it to that man. Promise me you'll keep it."

"I don't plan to leave," I say. "Or sell. Cole and I will likely split it like a vacation home."

The women exchange unreadable glances, then Lily turns toward the house again with a sad smile. "Well, we wish you could be our neighbor permanently, but I think she'd like knowing you're here in whatever way you can be."

I want to tell her she's wrong—clearly. That I was just

the only choice she had when she was looking for someone to leave the house to. But I don't want to sully her memory of Vera, so I say nothing.

"You should change the passcode to the gate, by the way," Jane says. "So you don't have to worry about him coming back."

Intrigued, I study her. "Actually, do you know how to do that?"

She gives me a prize-winning smile. "I most certainly do."

CHAPTER EIGHTEEN

BRIDGET

After we change the gate code and say goodbye to the neighbors, Cole and I make our way up the lawn and toward the front porch. Some of my fear from this morning has dissipated, though so many of my thoughts are still overloaded with worry—an echo chamber of ever-present panic.

There's a dead body in the backyard.

Oh, that's a pretty flower.

Vera killed your parents.

Cole has been really nice lately.

Vera killed someone and buried them in the yard.

I should make something for the neighbors as a thank you for being so kind.

I was staring at a skeleton less than an hour ago.

When we reach the porch, I freeze.

It's impossible, and yet, there it is.

Another letter. Two in one day. That's never happened before.

Cole grabs it first but hands it over to me when I reach for it without a scene. I tear it open. This is starting to feel cruel. I'm not sure how much my heart can take or how I'll survive another soul-crushing secret.

Dear Bridget,

For all of Vera's secrets, this house has a secret too. Before you make any decisions, I need to show it to you.

In the basement, in the far corner of the room, you'll find a metal door built into the floor. During prohibition, the tunnels were used to transport liquor to and from the town center. Before that, there were many rumors about what they were used for. Now, most people have forgotten they exist.

Not everyone, though.

Vera knew about the tunnels, and they helped her commit some of her most atrocious crimes. Don't believe me? Go check.

Signed,
A friend

I glance at Cole, who's reading the letter over my shoulder.

"Tunnels?" I ask with a sigh. "Seriously?"

He scratches his eyebrow in thought. "Have you ever been in the basement?"

"No. I know there is a basement, but Vera made it clear that it was off limits. It floods really badly when it storms, and she was always worried about rats and mold. She said it was dangerous."

His brows jerk upward. "And you still want to go check it out?"

"Don't you?"

"Well, you're really selling it here, I've gotta tell you."

"Come on. We have to, don't we? That's the whole reason we're here. The reason we haven't called the police."

"I'm teasing. I'm obviously in if you are." He pulls open the door and we step inside. "Lead the way."

I head toward the hall and turn left, making my way toward the laundry room and guest bath, then down a smaller hall with two doors. One is just a broom closet. The other leads to the basement.

Cole stares at it strangely. "I can't believe you never tried to look down here."

"Vera told me not to. Besides, I'd seen enough scary movies that creepy, old basements didn't interest me in the least." I eye him. "Why? Did you go down here?"

He shakes his head. "I never really explored the house. Mom made it clear the areas I was allowed to go in: the yard, the bedroom I was given, and the common areas. If I snooped, she could've lost her job, so I stayed where I was allowed to be."

The words hurt my heart. Until this week, I'd never

spent much time thinking about how life must've felt for Cole while he was here. Like a prisoner, almost. That's how it seems. Like this was his cage, but he was never allowed to fully make it his home.

Vera could've done more to make him feel welcome. She should've done more.

And so should I.

The truth weighs heavily on me. I should've done more. I should've been kinder. I shouldn't have let my own issues cloud my judgment of Cole.

Reaching for the handle, I pull the door open. It sticks at first, and I have to wiggle it a bit, but eventually it gives.

The musty smell and warm, humid air hit me quickly, the humidity sticking to my skin. The room is dark, and I use the flashlight on my phone to search for a light switch on the walls, though there's nothing to be found.

Over my shoulder, Cole sucks in a breath. "Do you think there's a light down there?"

"Maybe." I'm trying to sound braver than I feel.

"I can go check. You stay here."

"No way," I say firmly, shoving one of my trembling hands into my pocket. "I'm going."

He nods. "Fine. I'm right behind you."

The wooden steps groan under our weight, and I have to wonder when someone might've been down here last. From the way it smells, I'd say it's been a long time since anyone opened that door, but then again, maybe basements just smell that way. We didn't have one in my parents' house, and

I don't have one in my apartment, so I wouldn't honestly know.

The darkness surrounds us as we descend into it. Cole stays close behind me, a hand on my shoulder as we make our way down the stairs. When we reach the bottom, I scan the space, my heart pounding in my ears as I wait for someone to jump out and grab us.

Finally, my eyes land on a metal string in the center of the room, and I bolt for it. The sharp *zzzzzing* of the cord fills my ears, and the room illuminates suddenly. The single bulb doesn't do much for the large space and everything is still cloaked in shadows, but it's better than nothing.

For the most part, the concrete room is empty. There's a stack of chairs leaning against a wall next to what looks like an old card table. A sofa sits against a different wall with a cream-colored canvas drop cloth over it.

The floor has a few wet spots on it, and there are plastic containers stacked around the room in random places with Vera's familiar, large, loopy handwriting on them: *Christmas. Fall. Home movies. Harold.*

The 'home movies' container catches my eyes first, and I open it, but I find that everything inside is on VHS. I pick up a few tapes and read the descriptions, her handwriting hitting me with a pang of nostalgia.

Christmas 1988
Jenn's 16th
Summer of 1972
Beach Trip 1978

Bitter Corp Christmas Party #32
Chrissy's Graduation
Senior Prom
Jenn's Wedding
Chrissy's Wedding

I sort through a few more, sad that we have no way to watch them anymore. The memories have nearly been lost to time and technology. It makes my heart ache just a bit to think that my mom exists within them, and I make a mental note to find a VHS player on eBay so I can watch them soon.

I shove those containers out of the way, searching the floor until I spot one with my name on it. A golf ball lodges in my throat, unmoving no matter how hard I try to swallow it down.

I lift the lid and look down inside, my eyes welling with tears.

Patricia. My baby doll with the wonky eye that would never quite open right. I'd nearly forgotten about her. I smooth the dusty, blue dress and her wild, dark hair, holding the plastic form to my chest as I continue to search. There are drawings and letters I wrote to my parents, my handwriting getting progressively better over the years. I find stacks of photographs of me throughout the years—years before I came to Bitter House, when I was still with Mom and Dad. There's a bit of extra light in my eyes then. Even if I didn't know how old I was, I could tell you it was before they'd passed with a single look.

A stuffed rabbit sits near the bottom of the bin. *Bun Bun.*

Why did Vera keep all of this? Why didn't she tell me it existed? How could she keep things that had once belonged to my mom if she knew she was the one who had killed her? I want to take this as a sign that the letter writer is wrong. That my instincts about Vera, about how she could never actually hurt my mom, are right. Maybe the person writing the letters wanted to prove they were right about one thing so I'd believe them about everything else without questioning them too much.

Or...maybe not.

Or maybe it's all true.

Vera should've given me these things when I turned eighteen. She should've sent it with me when I left, so I had pieces of my parents. Whatever remained of them.

Still, I have to be at least somewhat grateful that she kept them and left me the house. If she'd left it to Aunt Jenn, I have to believe it all would've been tossed out.

One good deed to make up for all the bad.

"I found something." Cole's voice draws my attention from the corner of the room where he's been moving stuff, noisily sliding the plastic containers across the concrete floor.

I jerk my head around to look at him, and by the worried expression on his face, I know what he's found: the door in the floor, just like the letter said.

I cross the room toward him quickly as he shoves the last of the stacks of containers out of the way, staring down while he scratches his temple. When I near him, I see it. A rusting, round, metal door sits on the floor near the corner, previously covered up by the containers.

He bends down, giving me a questioning look before he jerks at the handle. The door releases a dull groan as the metal hinges give way. I take the door from him, pulling it open the rest of the way and laying it back against the floor. Together, we stare down into the darkness.

His eyes meet mine. "Now what?"

CHAPTER NINETEEN

VERA BITTER

When we moved into Bitter House, Harold told me about the tunnels. Rumor has it, they once connected most of the houses in the city, and even to some businesses, banks, and the courthouse. Of course, the Bitters being one of the most prominent families in the city, they have firsthand knowledge of it all. Stories that have been passed down from father to son over years and years. A long time ago, they were used to take deposits from businesses to the banks without having to go through town. When Prohibition came, though it was never truly enforced in Nashville, alcohol was smuggled back and forth through the tunnels. Some of the tunnels were used to transfer dead bodies from the hospitals to the universities for research and study. And, of course, criminals used the tunnels for their own dirty deeds.

Eventually, most of the tunnel ends were sealed. Some paths were damaged or caved in throughout history, and plenty of areas became unsafe. But Bitter House's remained in perfect condition. Quite handy for Harold and his friends to play in when they were younger and sneak out when they were older.

And, of course, they became *quite* convenient for me as well.

In public, women are often invisible, harmless, unless they're drawing attention from the male gaze. But I was never invisible. Not as a young girl, not with the way I looked—it's not bragging, I'm just honest. Not when I was older and married to one of the richest men in the city. And not now, now that I'm older, widowed, and an enigma.

So, traveling in secret is important. Secrets are the most powerful thing a woman owns.

It was the tunnels I used the first time Reggie hit me. And again the night I decided to do something about it. The ladies next door—Jane, Cate, and Lily—have become my closest confidants. When he hit me, I went to them. I have no idea why, even now when I think back on it. We weren't friends. We'd hardly spoken more than a dozen words to each other since we became neighbors, but still...there was a knowing. Most women have it, though I wish it were all of us. A sense that we're in this together. That it's never been us against us, but always us against them.

So, I went to Jane first, who called Lily and Cate, and we formulated a plan. They helped me escape through the tunnels, get my most important possessions out, and then helped me hide away while we called the attorney to get the annulment drafted. My attorney told him we hadn't been married long enough for him to claim any of the money in my name, so the measly check I offered him was enough to send him packing.

Of course, when I came back, the house was a mess. He'd destroyed things—priceless things. He'd torn paintings, stolen family heirlooms, broken tiles, and torn light fixtures from the walls. He'd taken a hammer to the dry wall and urinated in our bed.

It was a small price to pay to have our home free of him, to have my girls safe.

It was a painful and expensive time, but it was important. I see that now. It showed me how good Harold was and how strong I am.

Which is why...I did what I had to do, in the end.

I didn't have a choice.

I was tired, honestly. Tired of seeing women being torn down by men. Tired of seeing men walking around like that thing between their legs means they can control the world and no one will ever stand up to them. I got tired of being the woman who didn't stand up.

Money gave me power, sure. Power most women didn't have. And what about them? They were just supposed to take it?

When Edna came to work for me, I knew.

I knew in the way I know when a storm is coming, or how I can sense tension when I walk into a room. I could feel it when I met her. She was all at once just like me and nothing like me.

She was scared.

She was trying.

But she was poor. Her options were limited.

I'd never had a house manager live with me before, but I offered the option to her one day, just out of the blue. I'm not sure I realized I even had the idea until the words were out of my mouth.

You should move in with me.

I had the space, after all. And it did make her job easier. Plus, here within the walls of Bitter House, I promised her she'd be safe. I didn't have to explain what that meant. We understood each other in a way only women who've experienced abuse can.

The next day, Edna and Cole moved in with me. He was a scrawny little thing. Hardened by all he'd seen. Quiet. He reminded me so much of my girls when they were young— all elbows, knees, and wild feelings. Of course, he also came with a broken heart. We weren't so different in that way. I wanted more than anything to protect him. To protect them both.

And so...I did.

For a while, things were okay. Safe. Happy. We settled into a new normal and became a little unit.

The day Don came to the house, everything changed.

He wasn't going to leave, not without his wife and son. That's what he told me. As if they were his property. That's the problem with men like that. They think the entire world belongs to them.

I'd wanted to keep her safe. I'd hired an attorney for her to help with the divorce. I'd told her my story, eventually.

But it wasn't enough. He was at my door, and I knew

then from the look in his eyes, even if I kept her locked inside my house, Don wasn't like Reggie. He didn't want money. He wanted them.

And I couldn't let that happen.

The first time I ever held my husband's gun was the night I killed a man. And I'd do it again.

In a heartbeat.

CHAPTER TWENTY

BRIDGET

We stare down into the dark hole in the ground. The air is cool and musty, more earthy than the basement. I'm brought back to digging up the garden grave, the way the mud seemed to permeate my every sense. I can feel it between my teeth as if I'm the one buried.

"Should we go down there?" I ask.

"No," Cole says, too quickly. "No. We have no idea what's down there. It's not the basement. There could be snakes or rats, and that's the best-case scenario."

I swallow. "What's the worst?"

His dark eyes meet mine slowly, almost like he doesn't want to look at me. "That whoever is writing these letters is counting on us going down there. Whether that's because they're down there waiting on us or they know what is, I'm not sure. But we can't go down there, Bridget." He uses his phone's flashlight to scan the ground below us. A small metal ladder leads the few feet to the damp ground. There are cobwebs in every direction, gnats flying toward the light. He sticks his head into the tunnel, shining the light this way and that. "Besides that, the tunnels could collapse. We have no idea how old this is or where it leads."

"Maybe it's not a tunnel at all. We can't see far into it. What if it's, like, a safe room or a storm cellar?" I suggest as the idea occurs to me. "In a house like this, they probably had the money to install something like that."

"A storm cellar, maybe, but still, they had the basement. It was sort of unnecessary. And if it's a safe room, I'd think there would be more precautions." He stands, leaning past me to close the door. "Either way, it's not safe."

"But the letter writer was right again."

He nods, and neither of us have to say anything for him to know I'm thinking about my parents now. I swallow, drying my eyes and smearing mud across my cheeks.

"We just have two more letters," I point out, looking down. "Once we have all the information, we'll tell the police everything."

"Agreed." He runs his foot across the door. "We should probably put the containers back over this. Just in case."

The insinuation is chilling: just in case someone from inside the tunnels were to try to get into our house. In case they climbed the ladder and pushed open the door. In case they walked into our house. Came for us. Killed us.

Suddenly I'm a child, picturing werewolves and slime monsters crawling up from the tunnel.

We push the containers back into place, weighing down

the door with several hundred pounds of stuff, and make our way back upstairs, leaving the light on this time.

I can't get to the shower fast enough.

That evening, I'm completely and utterly exhausted, and I use every chance I get to peer out the back windows to look toward the garden as if I expect to see the skeleton hand popping up from the dirt.

As I pull Jane's chicken enchiladas from the oven, the warm, delicious scent fills my nose, and I try to focus only on that. Cole is back at the dinner table, finishing up what he was working on this morning, when I carry our plates over to him and place them down.

He looks surprised when I set his meal in front of him.

"You made dinner?"

"Well, Jane made dinner. I heated it up." I sink into my chair across from him, and he closes his laptop before picking up his fork.

"Thank you."

I draw in one corner of my mouth. "I figured it's the least I can do after I dragged you on all of my adventures today."

His smile is soft and sort of lost, his eyes dancing between mine. "I never mind going on adventures with you."

"Even when they leave your hands looking like that?" I

point at his hands with my fork. The palms of both our hands are red and raw from digging.

He stares down at them but nods. "Even when my hands look like this."

"Such a gentleman," I tease, taking my first bite of casserole. It's too hot, so I strategically take deep breaths until I can swallow, the meal scalding my throat and chest as it goes down.

"I don't know about that," he says with a laugh. "Just a guy who always wanted his life to be a little more exciting."

I wave a hand around the room. "How do you get more exciting than this?"

His laugh goes from genuine to serious as it falls away. "How are you holding up, by the way? I know it's sort of weird with everything we've learned."

I set my fork down, taking a deep breath. "I still don't know what to believe, you know? On the one hand, everything the letter writer has told us is true, except what we can't prove, but on the other...I just don't want to believe it. I want to think I knew Vera. That I wasn't wrong to trust her. Even if I didn't always like her, I don't want to think she was capable of harming anyone—not physically anyway, but the proof is in the backyard. Maybe she fought with my mom over money. Clearly that's an issue with this family. Maybe it was an accident. Maybe things got out of hand, and—"

"Look," Cole says, his voice calm, "as far as we know, Vera had nothing to do with the body in the backyard. It could've been there for years before she was here. I don't know how this person knows about it, but it doesn't prove anything. And as far as thinking she might've hurt your parents, I just...I don't know, B. It doesn't make sense to me, you know? I know people do awful things to their family—to their kids—every day, but your mom was an adult, not a toddler who'd annoyed her. Vera wasn't a monster. Your parents died in a car accident. She would've had to plan that. Hire someone. It's not like she accidentally pushed her down the stairs in a moment of passion, you know?"

I swallow. He's right, but I don't know if that makes me feel any better.

"The police ruled it an accident, didn't they? Your parents?"

We've never really talked about them. Or about anything else, for that matter. "Yeah."

"Then let that be the truth you believe until we have proof otherwise. Until then, it's just a rumor."

When we've both finished eating, Cole cleans up the meal while I wash our dishes. It's funny how quiet the house feels now without Vera. Even before, I've only known this house with a few people in it—never a house full of people like the Bitters used to have, but her absence is felt in every moment.

I feel Cole move beside me, his arm brushing mine. A yawn escapes my lips as he brushes a piece of hair behind my ear, his thumb grazing over my cheek. "Soap." He smiles, pulling his thumb back to reveal a bit of suds.

"Oh." I rub my cheek again to be sure it's clean. "Thanks again for helping clean up. Me *and* the meal, apparently."

He folds his arms across his chest, leaning back against the counter. "We make a pretty good team, you know? I don't think it'll be so bad just sharing this place."

"Yeah, I've actually been thinking, and I don't know if I'll want to stay here after everything we've learned," I admit.

He nods, chewing his bottom lip. "I can't say that I blame you, but you should take some time to think about it. Don't make any rash decisions, okay?"

"What's there to think about?"

He studies the floor. "I don't know. I guess I just think... I mean, this house is yours as much as it's mine. As much as it was hers. And there are still plenty of good memories that have been made and will be made here, you know?"

"Good memories, hmm?"

"Yeah."

"For example?"

"Well...what about that time we danced in the kitchen?"

"Danced?" The word feels completely foreign and out of place. I have no idea what he's talking about.

He takes hold of my arms without warning, pulling me to him playfully, and begins spinning us around, dipping me backward. I laugh and roll my eyes. "This time, remember?" he teases.

"Ah, yeah, now it's ringing some bells." I wrap my arms around his neck just as he looks down at me, and suddenly, the air in the room shifts. We're nose to nose, our lips nearly touching. His eyes dance between mine with words unspoken, and when he opens his mouth, I feel his breath on my skin. If either of us tilts our chins forward even just a little bit, I'd finally know what it feels like to kiss him.

Before I can seriously contemplate making the move, he chuckles, dropping his hands down away from my waist, but he doesn't step back. "Sorry about that."

"About what?" I ask, my voice sounding bolder than I feel.

"Um." He swallows. We're so close in the kitchen that I swear I can feel his heartbeat, our chests touching. With each inhale, he presses against me. He brushes hair back from his eyes, opening his mouth. His dark eyes heat with something dangerous. "I just..." He blinks and looks away. "My point is...don't let her take anything else from you."

I swallow, unsure if he's talking about the house or... something—someone—else. My stomach flips at the thought. When did I stop hating him? When did he start feeling less like an enemy and more like a friend? What if he's just tricking me so he can keep the house?

With that worry plaguing me, I can no longer focus on how good he smells or how much I like the feel of his hands on my skin. Chills creep down my spine, and I step back, clearing my throat.

The smile dies on his lips.

"Where'd you go?" he asks. "Did I do something or—"

"I should get to bed," I say, cutting him off. I don't know what's coming over me or why I'm suddenly incapable of controlling my thoughts around this man.

I can't trust anyone but myself, I know this. Before I can change my mind, I dart from the room.

CHAPTER TWENTY-ONE

BRIDGET

The next morning, before I've even brushed my hair or changed into clothes, I race down the stairs and swing open the door. It's starting to feel like Christmas with gifts I don't want, but I also can't resist.

When I spot the welcome mat, my heart sinks. There's nothing there. No letter, no security camera box, which was supposed to also have been delivered last night.

That's when I remember—the gate code.

Shoot. My heart plummets. I changed the code yesterday but forgot to update it in the delivery app. When I look ahead, I can vaguely see a hint of something brown attached to the iron gate—the letter is there waiting for me.

Without hesitation, I slip on my shoes and rush down the driveway as fast as my legs will carry me. When I reach the gate, my heart is racing in my chest, both from exertion and adrenaline.

The letter has been taped to the front of the gate—the

sender couldn't get inside. I pass by the motion sensor, causing the gate to slowly start opening, and squeeze through the small crack before it can swing open the rest of the way.

Quickly, I tear the letter from the gate and rip open the brown envelope, reading the words waiting for me.

Bridget,

By now, I hope you trust that I am trying to help you. I've been honest with you about almost everything. There are, however, a few lies I need to correct, and I hope you'll understand why I had to tell them. The first is merely a lie of omission. You see, while I promised you just one more letter after this one, I'm sure you have several questions for me that can't be answered with just these two letters. Therefore, in addition to the next letter, I will give you something that I hope will answer more questions than I could. I thought you should hear the truth from Vera herself. Check the panel in the back of her top dresser drawer. I will tell you the second lie, and the final secret, very soon.

Signed,
A friend

I read the letter again, skimming to the important parts, then look around. What could the letter mean? How on earth will I get to hear this from Vera herself?

My mind goes instantly to the tapes in the basement. Will there be a recording of her somehow? A home movie? Was Vera the type of serial killer who recorded her crimes? Does that sort of killer even exist?

If it is a videotape, I won't have a way to watch whatever I'm meant to see until I find a way to play it, which is proving challenging. I spent a few hours last night scrolling through online listings for VHS players, but I found very few to choose from.

On the ground near the edge of the driveway, propped up against the brick pillars framing the gate, I spot a brown box that tells me exactly what I expected. Without the correct code to get inside, the delivery driver who was dropping off the security camera was left with no choice but to put the package here.

I scoop up the box and hurry back toward the house.

Inside, I place the camera package on the table so I don't forget to install it soon, before the next letter has a chance to arrive. I want to set it up this morning, just in case we receive the last letter this afternoon, two in one day like we did yesterday. Unless they eventually reveal themself, we only have one more chance to catch the sender in the act. We'll have to figure out where to place the camera so we can see the gate, rather than the front door now, and with the long driveway, that could be a challenge. Before I can do anything else, though, I have to find out what this current letter is talking about. What secret is lurking in the back of Vera's dresser?

It feels weird to be searching for answers without Cole, but I don't want to bother him. After the way we left things last night, the air is buzzing with awkwardness and tension.

Besides, I'm independent, and I can do this. If there's one thing Vera taught me, it's that I don't need a man to be powerful. To be in control. To be safe.

Back in her room, I shove the letter into my back pocket and head for the closet. She has two dressers in here—a long one with two sets of three drawers, and a tall one with five drawers. The letter didn't specify which one, but since it said top drawer and only one has a single top drawer, I go for the tall dresser first.

I pull open the drawer to find several silk bras and reach toward the back. My hand stops halfway, and I realize this drawer is much shallower than it should be. Upon closer inspection, I realize that—*yes!*—the drawer is half as deep as the dresser. I push on the panel gently, moving my fingers around the edges as I try to peer in the drawer, head tilted to the side and one eye closed.

When I press on the upper-left corner, the panel pushes in, then rebounds and jerks back toward me with a click as if it's on a spring, similar to the hidden panel in the wall behind me. Carefully, I nudge it again, and as the panel drops down, I reach my hand farther back until my palm connects with something soft and cold. I know what it is instantly: *a book.*

I pull it out to confirm that I'm right, turning it over in

my hand. The cover is red and nondescript. Simple. Genuine leather with intricate patterns.

I open to the first page, smoothing my fingers over her writing—the familiar look of the large loops and swirls of her letters.

This journal belongs to:
Vera Bitter

CHAPTER TWENTY-TWO

BRIDGET

As mad as I am at her, the temptation to hear from Vera again is undeniable. The solace I find in seeing her handwriting disturbs me—I should not want to hear from her. She's a murderer. She lied to me. She kicked me out.

But no matter how many times I repeat these things in my head, the truth is there, as real as the heartbeat in my chest: I want her to prove me wrong. And somehow, I know that she won't. I know that she's going to let me down once again. Just like I've always known whoever is writing me these letters knows the truth about everything.

Somewhere deep in my core, like a piece of fruit rotting, I've felt it. I've felt the way my entire world is getting ready to crumble. I'm on the precipice of it all falling apart.

I sink onto the carpeted floor of her closet, turning to the first page, and with a deep breath, I begin to read.

I was never sure about changing my last name after I was married. Isn't that funny? In those days especially, it was unheard of for a woman to think of such things. But I was a Shuffle, had been all my life. My daddy was a Shuffle and his daddy and so on, and I guess in some strange way, it felt like giving up the last piece of myself if I chose to do it.

...if I'm being honest, I loved the weight the last name carried. Being a Bitter in this town, I might as well be a Rockefeller or a Kennedy.

...I can still picture it now, if I try. The way that smile made me feel could be studied. Books could be written about it. But...like all the best stories, it had to end. And, when it did, I was grateful I had the Bitter name. Because that's exactly what I was: bitter.

...Reggie came along when I was still trying to find my place. I've always been a stubborn child. Momma and Daddy used to say I'll be too stubborn to die one day, and I have no evidence to the contrary.

...she was scared. She was trying. But she was poor. Her options were limited.

...the first time I ever held my husband's gun was the night I killed a man. And I'd do it again. In a heartbeat.

My heart stops as I read those words. The admission in Vera's own hand. She was a killer. Worse...she killed Edna's husband. Cole's dad. There were so many other possibilities of how to deal with the threat he posed. So many other ways she could have handled it. She said it herself: she was powerful. She could've made him leave. She could've had him arrested. Hired security to keep them safe. She had so many other options than the one she chose.

Then my chest turns to ice. *The man in the woods—the body—it might be Cole's dad.*

Oh god.

I feel sick. My stomach churns with the thought of it. The fingers, the bones he unearthed, could've been his own flesh and blood. How can I ever tell him?

Before I have my answer decided, I hear the bedroom door open farther. His light footsteps tap across the floor as he makes his way through the room, closing the space between us. I slam the book shut seconds before he appears.

When he does, his eyebrow quirks up. "Why are you on the floor?"

CHAPTER TWENTY-THREE

VERA BITTER

Don hasn't been the only one, of course. He was the first. The catalyst, though I hate to call him anything that sounds so important. I didn't ask Edna before I did it. Maybe I should have, but I think she would've said no. I took his life and didn't look back, didn't ask for forgiveness or permission.

I saved her unapologetically.

When I told her what I'd done a few hours later, she cried. To this day, I don't know if she was crying for herself or Don, or maybe me, but she did. It was understandable, obviously. What she'd been through, what she was going to go through in the future, was a lot.

I understood the loss and the pain with my whole heart, after Harold. But our grief was not the same. Don was a monster, and my Harold was far from it.

We buried Don in the backyard. Edna helped a little, but it was grueling work. It took over a week to dig the grave, with Don's body resting and waiting in the tunnels below the house. It kept him cool, but not cold. By the time we buried him, he was a nasty sight.

I still don't know how I managed it. I've always gotten nauseous when one of the girls had a bad cut, but with him, I was just numb. It was what had to be done, and so, I did it.

As simple and as complicated as that.

Since Edna, there have been others. Women I've met here or there. Women like us.

To be clear, it was never the plan. I didn't set out to do this.

I just...have.

I'm cautious about whom to trust, always. You have to be. The wrong one and it could bring everything down around us.

I've never wanted money. Hell, I have more than I could ever hope to spend. Money is meaningless to me. What I want, I'm discovering, is power. I want to feel like I'm doing something that matters.

I want to help people.

And I have the resources to make it happen.

It started with Cate's sister, whose husband had beat her around so badly she'd lost two babies during separate pregnancies. I'd had the girls over for drinks one night when Cate mentioned how much she wanted to kill him.

It was silly girl talk. Meaningless. A few glasses of wine, a loose tongue, a hidden desire.

I asked why she hadn't.

And that was that. It sounds simple, maybe, but sometimes I think all we need is permission.

We made a plan. Cate would have them over for dinner while Jane, Lily, and I snuck in and took care of him. Old women are invisible, after all, since men don't tend to want to take our clothes off. But we are stronger than we look. A whack to the back of the head. Smothering him in his state of unconsciousness. It was easier than the gun. Much less messy too.

And then...it nearly fell apart.

Cate was meant to keep her sister in the other room, but she heard the commotion. She couldn't stop her from coming in to see what we had going on.

She cried so hard when she saw him, but it wasn't for any of the reasons I'd suspected Edna's tears came. No, when Cate's sister got ahold of herself enough to catch her breath, she came right out with it: two days earlier, she'd found out she was pregnant. She hadn't yet summoned the courage to tell her husband. Most likely, we'd just saved her child's life.

That was a good feeling. The very best feeling. It made digging his grave that much easier. We helped her with her story—that Sal had run off with some woman he met in a club in Vegas. She was alone to raise her child, but more importantly, she was safe.

It felt good, diary. It felt better than I've felt in a long time.

And well, after that, we found our purpose.

Jane, Lily, Cate, and I—we are determined to make the world a better place in the only way we can: by getting rid of the men who make it worse. I wish I could say you'd be surprised at how many there are, but I don't think anyone would.

Women come to us through the secret network we've built—women who trust us and believe in us. Women who have no other options. It's easy to assume they do have other options—that they must—but until you've lived it, you couldn't possibly understand.

What sort of life is it to look over your shoulder constantly? To worry and stress, even if you get away, over when he'll find you? How much longer you have until he comes back?

The law doesn't protect us. Not fast enough, not strongly enough. So we have to do it ourselves.

CHAPTER TWENTY-FOUR

VERA BITTER

By protecting women, I've put myself in hell.

I thought by doing the right thing, I was somehow righting my karma for the money my husband's family has, for the privilege I undoubtedly carry.

Two weeks ago, I found out I saved them only to hurt myself. To tear myself apart at the seams and spread my body across hot coals.

These will be the hardest words I'll ever write: Christina, my sweet, sweet Chrissy, and Nathan are dead. And it's all my fault.

Six months ago, a woman came to us. She'd heard about what we do, and she needed us to take care of her husband. By now, we know our names have been passed around. Women come to Jane first, who seems to be able to judge their intentions best, then through the tunnels to Bitter House where we all gather to hear their stories.

We trusted her.

We believed her.

And she lied to us.

I can't blame her, not really, but I do. I do anyway. She was scared. She was in danger, and now she's dead. But so is my daughter.

She was afraid, she panicked, and at the last minute, she did what she swore she'd never do. She told her husband the truth. She told him everything—who we are, what we were planning, where to find us. We were supposed to meet them at a restaurant, where I'd drug his drink with a plant from my garden, and we'd take him back to Bitter House to get the job done, but they never showed.

Two weeks ago, Christina was in a car crash that claimed her life. My son-in-law's life. My world. Bridget only narrowly made it out with her life, but every part of it has been shredded. Her parents are gone, her childhood, her friends. She has moved in with me, and nothing in this world makes sense.

Today, the woman's husband visited me. He knew my house. Knew my name. Knew everything. He told me what he'd done—that he'd taught me a lesson. He'd followed my daughter and son-in-law and chased them off the road. Left them for dead. He'd killed his wife, too. Made her pay for what she'd nearly done to him.

And as my punishment, he left my entire world shattered. Lily, Jane, and Cate weren't targeted, and I can only assume it's because they don't have any close family. No kids, no spouses. No weaknesses. I'm a public figure. Effortlessly found. Just ask anyone around town, and you'll easily discover the names of everyone I know and love.

I did this to myself. I wanted too much.

I can't write more, just the facts. The man is gone. Out there somewhere. But this could happen again. I can't keep any of them close. Can't have family for anyone else to find.

Can't let them believe I care about anyone, myself included.

Honestly, I'm not so sure that's a lie anymore.

CHAPTER TWENTY-FIVE

BRIDGET

Cole stares down at me as if I've grown a second head. He bends down, looking at the journal, but doesn't try to take it from me. "What's that?"

"Just a book." I don't know why I lie, but it's the first thing that comes out of my mouth, so I go with it.

"You okay?"

"No, actually, I...I need to know something."

"Okay."

"What happened to your dad?" I blurt the words out.

He drops to the ground in front of me. "What?"

"Your dad. Where is he?" *How much did Vera tell him? Does he know? Has he been lying to me?* My world is crumbling.

"Um, I don't know. He ran off when I was little. Why?"

I swallow. "Really?"

"Yeah. I don't remember much about him, just that he was here one day and then...then he wasn't." He shrugs. "I was six at the time, so it's basically always been me and Mom." He pauses. "And Vera."

I pass him the book slowly. "I...I'm so sorry. I think you should read this."

His brows knit together as he turns it over. When he opens it, his eyes go wide. "Holy shit, is this real? Where did you find this?"

"It was hidden in a panel in the back of her dresser. We got another letter this morning with instructions for finding it."

Without waiting for me to say more, he begins to read. His eyes scan the pages, finger trailing over the words. I know when he's reached the part I'm waiting for because he stops. Rereads. Finally, he looks up at me, his face sallow. "They...she...they killed my dad?"

"Vera did," I correct. "Edna wasn't involved."

"He was... He hurt her? He hurt my mom?" His dark eyes line with tears I hadn't expected. Suddenly he looks so small and breakable, I can't resist the urge to reach for him. He pulls back when my hand touches his arm, as if the move is just as unexpected for him as it is for me. When our eyes meet, I see the small boy he was back then, broken and hiding so much. I see that we've always had more in common than I realized.

He blinks and tears cascade down his cheeks, but he brushes them away quickly, setting the journal on the ground.

"Cole, I'm so sorry."

"We don't even know that it's true," he says, looking

away. "We don't know anything. For all we know, whoever wrote these letters planted this journal full of lies here for us to find."

He wants—needs—to believe it, and I wish I could give that to him, but it's in Vera's handwriting. I would recognize it anywhere. "Maybe you should call your mom," I suggest softly.

His entire body turns to steel at the suggestion. Eventually, he looks my way. "You mean I should ask her if it's true? Tell her we know about it?"

I nod. "It's the only way to know for sure."

He pushes up from the ground, pacing. "How do I even...do that? How do I just ask her? How could I possibly bring that up?"

"Tell her we found Vera's journal," I say. "She already knows about the letters. We trust her." As the words leave my mouth, I'm struck by how true they are. Throughout all of this, I've trusted not only Edna, but Cole, with everything I've uncovered. It's only now I'm realizing that might've been a mistake.

He pulls out his phone, hands shaking, and I'm surprised when he puts it on speakerphone as the line begins to ring. Trust, along with a strange sort of gratefulness for that trust, slam into me, and unexpected tears sting my eyes.

"I can step out if you want some privacy," I offer, though it's the last thing I want to do.

He shakes his head but doesn't get the chance to respond before Edna answers.

"Hey, sweetheart."

Cole opens his mouth, but at first, no words come out. He looks down, clearing his throat.

"Cole?" she says, obvious concern in her voice. "Are you there?"

He looks as if he's turned to glass, and I'm worried that the truth of all of this will break him.

"Mom." His voice cracks, and I stand up, moving toward him without volition. I slip my hand into his, holding his arm with my other hand. To my surprise, he leans his body against mine. "I need to ask you something."

Her tone is more urgent now. "You're scaring me. Is...is everything alright?"

"Did my dad hurt you?" He squeezes his eyes shut as he says the words, like they physically pain him.

The line is eerily quiet, then we hear her suck in a breath. When she speaks, her voice is shaky. "Where did you hear that? Why are you asking?"

"It was in the most recent letter," he says. "The person said..." He pauses, thinking. "They said that Vera took us in because Dad was hurting you. Is that true?"

"I should come over," Edna says. "Let me come over, and we can talk this through, okay?" I hear the truth in what she isn't saying, in the hurried, panicked cadence of her voice. The journal was right. The sender of these letters is right. And they know terrible things, not only about Vera, but about Edna, too. Even if she didn't kill her husband, she knew about his death and didn't report it. She helped dig the grave.

"I need you to tell me the truth, please," he says. "Right now. It can't wait."

Her next breath is ragged. "Cole, please."

"It's true." He pushes out a breath, releasing me and moving across the room as he runs a hand through his hair. "Why didn't you tell me? Why did you lie?"

"Sweetheart, you were so young. I never wanted you to know or to look at your father that way. I didn't want you to think badly about him. I didn't want *myself* to think badly about him. I loved your father, Cole. I swear to you, I did. And we had you when we were so in love." She hesitates. "But...eventually something changed in him. He lost his brother, your uncle. You're too young to remember, but it was horrific. He started drinking, and...he changed." She draws in a shaky breath. "I tried to get him help. I tried to see him through it, to stick around, but it became too dangerous. He put me in the hospital twice before he broke your arm."

My entire body goes rigid as I watch Cole grow pale. "I broke my arm at school."

"That's what I told you when you saw the pictures years later," she says. "I'm so sorry, sweetheart. I should've gotten you away sooner, but I was weak. I...Vera is the reason—the *only* reason—we survived. She got us out of there when I wasn't strong enough. She made sure your father could never hurt us again, could never hurt *you* again. She is the reason we still have each other, and I will forever be grateful to her for that. You have to understand that I wish it could've been different. Leaving your father, lying to you, it was never what I wanted, but I know now that if we'd stayed, I'd be dead. And I hate to think about the person he would've turned you into." She sobs.

"Mom, please don't—" He can't finish his sentence as tears choke his own words.

"Please don't hate me," she begs.

"I don't," he says. "Of course I don't."

"You are my child, Cole. Mine. You got the best parts of me. Your father does not define you, do you hear me? You are kind and loving and compassionate. Where you came from, who you came from doesn't matter."

He brushes his palm across his cheek, drying his tears as quickly as they fall. "Mom, I need to go."

"Oh, please don't do tha—"

"I love you, okay?" His voice is so soft I almost don't hear it. "I just need a minute. I'll call you soon."

"I love you too. Please call me back." She's still crying as he ends the call, and the thought of her all alone breaks my heart, but right now, it's Cole who needs me.

I approach him from behind, dusting a hand over his back. He runs his palm over his face before he turns to look at me. "I came from a monster, B. My dad was a monster." He stares down at his own hands as if he might be guilty of the same thing. "What am I supposed to do with that?"

Without warning, he falls into my arms, not crying but just existing. Just breathing and letting me hold the weight of all he's learned.

"You came from the kindest woman I know," I tell him gently, rubbing his back. I don't know what else to say, though I wish there was more that I could. I want to comfort him, but I don't know how. I don't know how to do any of this. So we stand there in each other's arms, like it's the most natural thing in the world.

Eventually, when he pulls back, he says, "That was him, wasn't it? In the garden? The body we found was my dad."

I give a small, sad nod, feeling guilty for a crime I had no part in. "I think so, yeah."

He shakes his head, staring off into the distance. "I don't remember him, you know? Like, I remember that he existed, but I have no real memories of my parents ever being together. It was always just Mom and Vera." He puffs out a breath of air. "What are we supposed to do?" His hand swipes down his face, eyes wide as he looks my way again. "If we call the police about the body, if they figure out who it is, Mom could go to jail. This changes everything."

A rock settles in my stomach. He's right. These consequences go far past Vera now.

PART 3

CHAPTER TWENTY-SIX

VERA BITTER

It's been three years since my last entry. Truth be told, I wasn't sure I'd ever write again, but over the weekend I found this old journal, and my last entry broke my heart.

I was lost then, after losing Christina. Confused. Devastated. Broken.

I'm still lost, devastated, confused, and broken, of course. I'm a mother who's lost a child. A wife without a husband. I am a shell of who I once was, and I know I'll never get that part of me back.

But...I'm okay. I'm breathing. Day by day. I've turned my pain into fuel for the cause, rather than shutting it down and running scared. The man who killed my daughter is in the ground in the woods surrounding our house. No one suspects a thing.

Another important update since I wrote last: after Chrissy's death, it took me a long time to decide what I was going to do. I wanted to quit. I wanted to back down and lick my wounds and hide. I haven't slept well since that day. Since the day I learned that she was dead, and it was my fault. Most people would give up, would back down and realize they've caused harm to the people they love.

But I'm stubborn, remember? Few things keep me awake at night like the knowledge that I caused my daughter's death. But the one thing that has? The fact that if I give up, if I run away with my tail tucked, they win.

The bad guys, the monsters, they win.

Silence of the good is the weapon of the wicked. If I sit back and let this happen, let one bad man stop me from doing so much good, then he has won.

I will never live down the guilt over my daughter. If I could bring her back, selfishly, I would walk away from this life in a second, but I can't. The only thing that gives my soul a bit of respite is knowing that I am still doing the one thing I have control over.

I won't back down. I won't stop what I set out to do. To kill the rapists and murderers and abusers. The fathers and brothers and husbands and friends who wield their power and strength to hurt those who can't defend themselves. These last three years have reminded me of why this is important. Why what we do matters.

We have saved more lives than we've taken. Women, children, future women, future victims. I've never laid a finger on anyone who didn't deserve it, and that's how I sleep at night, knowing that I am a god in my own right, making life better in the only way I can.

I used to get so overwhelmed when I looked at all the evil

in the world, wondering how any of it could ever be fixed or made better, but I'm realizing now that even if I can't make it all better, I can make some of it better for a handful of people, and that's enough. It has to be enough.

As much as it kills me, I haven't spoken to my family in years. It's too big of a risk. If it means they have to hate me in order for me to keep them safe, then so be it.

Bridget is the only one I have no choice but to keep close. If I don't, she has no one. I have no idea where she would go, and I've heard too many horror stories now about those sorts of situations.

She will stay with me and out of trouble, close enough that I can keep an eye on her until she's old enough. But I'll hold her at arm's length, never letting her get too close because it would only make the inevitable hurt worse. Getting close to her will mean the day I send her away will break both our hearts, and right now, I can still hope to only break mine. Once she's old enough, the second she's ready, she'll have to go, too. Far away from me. Should anyone ever come for me to punish me for what I've done, I need them to believe I don't care about her.

But I do, diary. I'm watching this little girl grow up, and she reminds me so much of her mother. Sometimes I just sit and watch her, and it's as if we're in a different time and place altogether. It's a cruel sort of bliss in that way.

Cole and Bridget are safe here, protected by Edna and me, as well as Jane, Lily, and Cate. The kids can never find out what we do, though. No one can.

Well, I suppose that's not true. Edna knows everything,

but she wants no part of it. She's too soft for this life. But she's a better mother to my granddaughter than I could ever be, and that's more than I could ask for.

She takes care of my home and my family, while I take care of the world. Take care of making sure someday the world will be just a little bit better for Bridget. Really, I think that's all I'm hoping for.

Isn't that what we're all hoping for? To leave the world a little brighter for our daughters? A little safer?

As I get older, as I see more, it's difficult to remember that. To remember why I do this, especially on the hard days when all I want to do is scoop Bridget up and run away with her, take her someplace where I can protect her forever. Where it's just me and her and none of the evil that exists in the world.

The logbook was Lily's idea, and I have to admit, it has helped. I pull it out from the secret place whenever I need a reminder. Names, reasons. Proof that I've done some good with this one, simple life.

But will it ever be enough? If I've saved the world and it's cost me my soul?

CHAPTER TWENTY-SEVEN

BRIDGET

"Okay, well, first thing's first, we have to know everything," I say, pulling the journal back from where it lies on the ground. I turn to the last page we were on and keep reading Vera's story.

The entries are heartbreaking and eye opening, flipping everything I thought I knew about Vera on its head. She was nothing like I thought. I judged her, misunderstood her. I couldn't see her pain through my own.

My eyes brim with tears when I read the kind things she says about me, about us. I just wish I'd known before she was gone. I wish I could've heard this from her in the flesh.

When I come to an entry that talks about a logbook, I read it twice. *Names, reasons...*

...I pull it out from the secret place.

Another secret.

Cole reads it a few seconds after I have, his finger shooting out toward the page as he reads the words aloud.

He looks at me, eyes wide. There's still a sadness there, an emptiness that hurts somewhere deep inside me, but it's been replaced by curiosity. Even as broken as he is by what we've discovered, he wants to learn more. "A logbook?"

"Hidden in a secret place. Was there anything else in the hidden place in the wall where we found the gun?" I ask him.

He shakes his head but moves toward the panel to check. "I don't think so." He eases Vera's boots out of the way and feels for the panel, pressing in on the wall when he finds it. The moveable piece of the wall leans in, allowing him space to reach his hand forward into the darkness. His hand searches in the shadows before I move toward him with my phone's flashlight, scanning the small space. "Nothing," he says after a moment. "What about where you found the journal?"

I shake my head. "It was really small. I don't think there'd be room for anything other than this, but I'll double-check too." I stand and cross the room, pulling open her drawer and pushing the panel back to search. I run my hand across the entire space, but I find nothing. "There has to be somewhere else. Another secret hiding place."

"I'd bet Vera has hiding places all over this house," Cole agrees, sounding wary.

"Yes, but the closet seems to be where she's hiding most of the important stuff. We need to check everywhere."

He appears dubious but doesn't argue. Instead, he sets to work examining the wall while I turn back to the dresser. I press against the backs of each drawer then scan underneath the dresser and along the bottom, searching for anything that might look suspicious, but I only find dust and cobwebs. I move to the other dresser and do the same, then search the backs of both.

Nothing.

I begin to check the carpet, searching for any loose or bumpy parts. When Cole is done checking the wall, we move to the bedroom, checking underneath her mattress and behind her nightstand.

But still, we find nothing. I pull at random books on her bookshelves, thinking it might be like the movies where touching the right book reveals a secret passageway, but nothing opens up. There is nothing, not even a hint at what Vera might be talking about.

Eventually, Cole sighs. "We should read more. Maybe she eventually tells where it's hidden. Otherwise, we're looking for a needle in a haystack."

I agree, but as my eyes fall on the clock, I gasp. It's just past noon.

Shoot.

"We need to install the camera," I tell him. "It came at some point last night, and if anyone drops off a letter midday like they did yesterday, I want to be sure we catch them. Especially if there's a chance they might go to the police. You were right before. This all affects your mom now, too."

He nods. "Okay, how about this: I'll work on installing it, and you keep reading the journal. Deal?"

"Deal." I follow him out of the room and down to the dining room. He's solemn as he opens the camera box and

195

begins evaluating the pieces. I know there must be a million things running through his head, thoughts and emotions I can hardly fathom, but he's clearly trying not to show it. I reach forward and squeeze his hand just once, and he squeezes mine back, not looking up, before I take a seat and open the journal.

I wonder where in the house Vera wrote the most? Did she ever sit in this exact spot? I can't imagine so, with people always around, but maybe. I try to recall ever seeing this book, but I can't.

This was another piece of her life she kept hidden from me.

Turning the pages, I search for the last entry I read, and my heart sinks. "There are only two more entries," I tell him softly. "Then she stopped writing."

"What?" He pauses what he's doing, staring at me. "Are you sure?"

I flip through the back of the journal so he can see what I can. Most of the pages here are still blank. Without saying another word, I start reading, stopping only when I've finished the first entry.

"She sent us away to protect us," I whisper, clutching my heart. Tears brim my eyes.

"Read it to me," Cole says, unscrewing the back of the camera.

I clear my throat and begin reading Vera's words aloud, choking up several times and having to stop to compose myself. When I'm done rereading the entry, I look up at him.

"She sent me away to protect me. It was never because she..." I can't finish the sentence, though I do in my mind.

Because she didn't love me.

Because she didn't want me.

Because she wished I'd never moved in.

Because she finally didn't have to pretend anymore.

He nods, seeming to understand without the words, but he doesn't push me to fill in any more. "What's the last entry say?"

"Right. Here we go." I turn the page and begin to read.

CHAPTER TWENTY-EIGHT

VERA BITTER

I'm back again. I know, I know, it's been a while. Six years, give or take. Sue me. I've been busy. It's strange how much time I don't seem to have anymore. After Harold died, it felt like the days were endless, like I could sleep for hours or weeks and mere minutes had passed.

Now, it seems I wake up and then, before I know it, it's dinner time and the day is ending. Having a child in the house again will do that to you, I suppose. Well, two children, really.

Edna and I are on our toes with those two, though Bridget is a good child. I don't worry about her as much as I worry about Cole. He's got young women parading through here all the time, but he doesn't fool me a bit. I've seen the way he looks at Bridget. There's something there, even if they don't see it yet. And god knows, I'll be grateful if they don't see it until they're much, much older.

He's a good boy, though. Protective. He's saved me

twice. I never thought I'd rely on a man again, but I have to admit, I'll be sad when he's gone. When they both are.

I don't want to think about that just yet, so I'll think about something happier. The nights he saved me.

Several years ago, we had a husband to take care of, and he arrived early, alone, and at the wrong house. Talk about a winner. Said the wife had taken a fall, and he'd be coming to the dinner party alone. I tried to get him to go to Jane's like we'd planned, but he wasn't listening. Things got heated, and Cole walked in on us in the middle of the fight. He went and got Edna, and we deescalated things, got him to Jane's, and everything went as planned from there. If Cole hadn't come in, if I'd been left in that room alone with him, I might've had to kill him there to save us all, something I've vowed to never do when the kids are home. I never want them to know anything about this or to put them in any danger if I can avoid it.

When the man looked at Cole, got a good look at his face, I knew I'd do anything if it meant he could never hurt him. I would kill for that child. Have killed for that child.

That was a long time ago. The second time he saved me was just last week, when another winner of a husband arrived and Cole heard him yelling at me. He's older now, obviously, but still smaller than the man. That thought didn't seem to cross his mind, though. He charged at the man like a bull and stood in front of me until he chased him off. He walked away like it was nothing, probably didn't give it a second thought, but he saved me.

Saved Bridget, who was in the house too.

I'm not sure what we'd do without him.

It's a nice reminder, having him here. Proof there are still good ones left.

CHAPTER TWENTY-NINE

BRIDGET

I look up at Cole, who is working diligently and avoiding my eyes as if he's being paid to.

"You saved Vera?"

His brow furrows. "I mean, hardly. I told some asshole to go away, that's it. And the other time I ran and got Mom. Not exactly hero behavior."

I flip through the book to be sure there's nothing left, but that's it. "There's so much we still don't know," I say sadly. "Whoever wrote the letters must've thought there was more in her journal."

"And we still don't know who that is," Cole says, setting his screwdriver down. "But we're about to." He turns the camera around and makes his way to the door.

"We have to point it toward the gate," I tell him, remembering. "With the code changed, that's where they left the last letter."

I follow and watch as he stands on the porch, scanning the yard. Eventually, he mutters, "That might work."

Without explanation, he crosses the yard, heading down toward the gate and stopping when he reaches the large tree in the front yard. He uses his drill to screw the camera's base into the bark of the tree, testing it for stability before he attaches the camera and points it toward the gate.

I always thought Vera was old-fashioned about safety out of personal preference, but now I'm realizing it must've been because she could never chance having video proof of who was at her house.

She put her own safety at risk for the women she saved. Even if I never get the logbook, even if I never get to know their names, it still means something. It's a reason to be proud of her, a reason to look deeper at every interaction we ever had.

He finishes with the camera quickly and turns to face me with a grin, but when he does, I'm standing too close. He nearly runs into me, but he steadies himself with a hand on my waist. Heat erupts under my skin surrounding his touch, as if I'm an icy window and he's placed a warm palm against it, melting the frost.

"Sorry," he says, his eyes soft.

"Don't be," I tell him, my eyes locked on his. "And thank you. For this and for everything you've done for me this week."

"Don't mention it." He still hasn't taken his hand off my waist. "Bridget, I—"

"Listen—" I say at the same time.

We laugh. "You go first," he says.

"I just wanted to say I'm sorry. I hate that you had to learn the truth about your dad this way. And I'm sorry that Vera did what she did. That she took away the chance for you to ever have him in your life, if that's what you wanted."

His eyes are serious as he stares at me. "I'm not upset at Vera. She saved my mom. And me, I guess. I wish I could've thanked her for that, eventually. It sucks that it happened, yes, but would I want it to have gone any differently? I don't think so."

I swallow, and his gaze moves to my neck. Then my mouth.

"Thanks for being here for me." His thumb circles on my hip. "Even though you hate me." There's nothing teasing about his tone; instead, it's as if he's tempting me to confirm what we both know.

"I don't hate you."

"Oh yeah?" He pulls his bottom lip into his mouth, scraping it with his top teeth. "Care to prove it?" Heat swoops through me, pulling somewhere deep in my core.

"How would I do that?"

He pulls me closer to him until our bodies are touching. "I have a few ideas." I roll my eyes, trying to regain my composure, and he laughs. "You should know, Vera wasn't wrong before," he says gently. "She may have taken some liberties about me saving her life, but...when she said I had a thing for you when we were kids, she was right."

Lightning zips from my fingers to my toes and everywhere in between. "She was?"

"I had no idea what I was doing when it came to you back then, B, and I regret it every day. But when I told you the other day that I had a crush on someone a long time ago, that I thought I loved her..."

There's so much meaning hidden behind his eyes, so much weight in the tone of his voice that I feel his emotion in my chest. His gaze rakes over me heatedly, and I can feel it, soft as a caress. "Yes?"

He sighs, cocking his head to the side. "Come on. Of course it was you. You knew it was you." His words land in my chest, spreading warmth everywhere.

I blink at him. "You never said anything. How would I have known?"

His hand lifts slowly to cup my cheek. "I couldn't say anything. Believe me, I tried. You were the one girl I couldn't...I don't know. Whenever I was around you, I lost it. You have no idea how many times I stood outside your bedroom door with this whole speech prepared, and...every single time, I chickened out. I had no idea what I was doing, but I knew I wanted you, even back then."

My chest tightens as my gaze falls to his lips. He runs his tongue over the bottom one. "Do you still feel the same way?"

There's a release of breath that sounds as if he's been holding it in, like he couldn't let it out until he finally told the truth. "I never stopped."

Without thinking, I lean forward, wrapping my arms around his neck. I pull him in for a hug, simple and sweet, until it isn't. Every part of my body feels every part of his. I can't breathe. Our skin is fused, our hearts racing. He's so close and smells so good, and suddenly, I'm forgetting everything else.

When we pull back, he doesn't let me go far. His eyes fall to my lips and this is a mistake, but it isn't, and I've never wanted anything so much.

His lips take mine gently at first, and then everything flips. His hand goes to the back of my head. It's possessive and crushing. He backs me into the tree until my body scrapes against the bark, his hands smoothing down my sides and back up like he can't explore fast enough.

He peppers my neck, jawline, and collarbone with kisses, his body putting constant pressure on mine as if he's afraid letting me go will break the spell.

"We shouldn't do this," I whisper. Even as I say it, my hands slide under his shirt, and he steps back, pulling it over his head.

"Definitely not." He shakes his head, staring at me as if I'm a mirage or a dream. As if he's still not sure any of this is happening.

His lips are back on mine in a second, and my heart beats so hard, so loudly, I feel as if I might pass out.

This isn't the time.

This could all be a trap.

My usual panicked thoughts are there, begging me to stop this, but I don't want to. I can't.

He picks me up with force, pinning me between him and the tree again. "Tell me to stop, and I will," he whispers, "but otherwise, I'm going to take you inside now."

"What for?" I ask, blinking up at him with desire pulsing through my veins.

He groans from somewhere deep in his throat, looking up toward the sky. "You need me to spell it out for you?" He's already walking, moving us toward the house.

"Maybe," I whisper, my voice needy as I drop my mouth to his neck. I kiss him the way he kissed me, tasting his skin. He picks up the pace, pushing us inside through the front door and into the living room. He pins me against the wall, his hands dropping to pull my shirt over my head.

"I want you, B. I've wanted you for as long as I can remember." He sets me down on the ground, trailing kisses down my front. "Your kisses, this fucking body—" He stops, pulling the cups of my bra down so he can pull my breast into his mouth. My body arches off the wall, and I cry out, unable to stop myself. He returns to my mouth briefly, claiming it, then goes back down, his tongue trailing a path from my ribs to my stomach, not stopping until he's reached the waist of my pants.

"Tell me to stop, or I'm not going to," he utters, lips hardly moving, dark eyes staring up at me. His touch is light and painfully teasing. I can't breathe. I'm suddenly sure I might die if he stops.

"Don't you dare stop," I say, running my hands through his hair. The air around us is electrified as I pull his dark locks through my fingers.

A wicked smirk crosses his lips as he drags my pants down. "That's my girl."

A hot ache grows in my throat. "Then shut up and prove it."

"My pleasure." The words on his lips are pure sin.

My core is molten liquid as he eases my underwear aside and presses his mouth right where I need him. My heart races, dancing in my chest in an erratic rhythm. My knees go weak, and he's holding me up, his hands under each of my thighs as I cry out, holding his hair, prepared to direct him though he clearly needs no direction.

Our eyes lock, and my body ignites, half ice and half flame. The world seems to spin out of control, careening on its axis. Everything, everywhere, stops existing all at once. It's only us and this feeling.

We are all that is left.

I'm nothing but pure lust in his hands, against his skin, his mouth. All too soon, I cry out, my body going rigid with the kind of pleasure you feel in every nerve ending as it spirals through my body. He grins against me, triumphant and unrelenting, as the tremors pass through my every muscle, not stopping until the final bit of liquid fire vibrates from my body.

He stands up, crushing his mouth to mine, as he lifts me up again and carries us toward the stairs. With savage intensity and impressive concentration, he refuses to stop kissing me even for a second as we make our way upstairs.

In his room, he places me down on the bed and undresses quickly, his lips meeting mine with a dreamy intimacy. As he eases himself onto the bed over me and sinks down between my legs again, I can't help wondering why the hell we haven't been doing this all along.

Later, we're still lying in his bed as I run my fingers over the hair on his chest, tracing swirls in it, my mind dizzy with thoughts and emotions I can't quite process yet.

"So, I've been thinking," Cole says with a sigh.

"Oh? Do tell." I'm thankful for the distraction.

He grins, one hand propped up under his head. "We should stay."

The idea makes me sad in a sort of nostalgic way I don't understand. There are so many bad memories here. How can he even consider staying?

"It's the only way to save Vera's secret. And Mom's."

"Stay forever?" I ask. The idea is both confusing and terrifying. This place is one giant mystery, much like the woman who once lived here. "What if it's dangerous? So many bad things have happened here, Cole. I don't know if I could do it. This place feels cursed."

"No one dangerous has any reason to come here anymore. Vera is gone. Besides, we've got the camera and the gate. We can get an actual security system. I know this place has bad memories, but it has some good ones, too. It brought us together, and...it protected us in ways we never knew. We could make it something special, you know? And keep the secrets safe."

I tap his chest thoughtfully. "There's a lot of 'we' talk going on right now."

He takes my hand in his and kisses my knuckles. "I'm not saying we have to live together as a couple or anything serious. I don't know what any of this means for us. All I'm saying is"—his eyes flick down toward mine—"I don't hate being here with you, and I don't want to give up the house Vera gave so much for. The house that protected the people we love."

"It wasn't the house," I say, though I know what he means. "It was Vera."

Before he can respond, we're interrupted by the sound of a doorbell.

CHAPTER THIRTY

BRIDGET

We dress quickly and rush down the stairs. No one has the new code. The delivery drivers couldn't make it through the gate, nor could anyone else. It's literally impossible for anyone to be here right now.

I'm still running my hands through my hair when Cole opens the door, and we spot Jane, Lily, and Cate standing there. It feels weird seeing them now when I've been reading so much about them in Vera's journal.

Do I tell them what I know? That we found Vera's journal? Do I tell them about the letters? Or do I pretend nothing has changed?

"Hey, ladies," Cole says, his voice deep and gravelly as if he's been sleeping.

They must've watched as I changed the code yesterday with their help.

"Can we come in?" Jane asks. "We need to talk to you about something serious."

The weight her voice carries makes my heart sink. *Something's wrong.*

Cole and I both mumble some variation of *yes* and *of course* and step back, allowing the women inside. They lead the way toward the sitting room, and we all take our seats, just like we did with Edna.

Once we're seated, Jane reaches into her purse. "I have something for you."

Before I can ask what she means or process what she's said, she produces an envelope that I recognize well. I stare at her outstretched hand, at the thick, brown paper. This one, like the first, has a red ribbon around it and is labeled with the number six. *The final secret.*

My gasp catches in my throat, eyes narrowing on her. "It was you."

She doesn't respond and simply taps the letter. "We'll explain, but first, you should read it."

All of the women are staring at me with unreadable expressions as I tear into the envelope with shaking hands. What will be the final, terrible secret? Why is Jane telling me all of this? Why did she write the letters?

I pull the letter from the envelope and unfold it, staring down at the paper. Confusion ricochets through me. "I don't..." I can't finish the sentence, can't make sense of what I'm seeing. Inside the envelope, I don't find the same font that has been used in all of the other letters. This time, as Cole leans over my shoulder to read the letter alongside me, I find the familiar large, loopy lettering of a handwriting I know by heart.

. . .

Bridget,

I hope you'll forgive me for the theatrics. Please know this wasn't done to torture you, but so you could hear an unbiased account of everything I've done.

So you could process everything, piece by piece. It is a lot to take in, and I know, had I chosen to tell you everything at once, how overwhelming it would've been.

By now, you know my secrets. You know that I was not a good person. That I was a murderer. That my choices are the reason your parents are dead. I could say 'I'm sorry' a hundred thousand times, and while it would be no less true, it would never be enough.

It has been the honor of my life to watch you grow up, my child. To love you from afar even when I had to keep you at arm's length. I hope someday you'll be able to accept, if not understand, why I did that. The day I sent you away was as painful as the day I lost Harold, and the day I lost your mother. Maybe more so because this time I had a choice. I'll never know if I made the wrong one. I saved lives, oh yes, but it came at the expense of your childhood, of your happiness and security, and if you never forgive me for that, I couldn't blame you.

When I knew I had little time left, I prepared these letters for you. I gave them to the women I trust most in the world—the women who are (hopefully) handing this to you now. Jane, Cate, and Lily are women you can trust with all your secrets, as I've always trusted them with mine. They will take care of you in a way that I no longer can, in a way I never truly could. I know you don't need that, my dear, but it gives me a sense of peace to think about you spending time with them. To think about you not being alone.

And speaking of alone, I hope you'll understand why I left the house to both you and Cole. Bitter House has always been yours, Bridget, always. But I knew losing me would come with a mixed bag of feelings, and stubbornly, I wanted to know you didn't have to deal with that on your own. I know you've had your issues with Cole in the past, but Cole and Edna are some of the only other people in the world I'd trust with you.

There are too many secrets out there. Too much danger. Keep your circle small. If there's any advice I can give you, it's that.

With the letters, I wanted you to finally have all the facts. I hoped you would wait to call the police until you knew everything, but I also knew you might not and that was a consequence we were all willing to deal with. The only bodies I told you about, the two in the garden—Don and the man who killed your parents—were ones that could be traced back to me and me alone. My friends would protect Edna, swear she couldn't have known about Don's murder. I also told them they could give you the letters sooner than just once per day if they worried you were dealing with too much stress.

Because this _is_ stressful, my darling, and I'm sorry to pass that torch to you. These are the secrets that eat away at you, and they are not your burden to bear. It is selfish of me to ask.

So, if you choose to walk away from it all, please know you have my blessing. But I hope you'll hear me out when I ask you to consider staying. To consider making Bitter House your home.

You don't have to hurt anyone, I want to make that clear. I would never ask that of you.

Jane, Cate, and Lily will take care of the men. They'll continue the legacy we built for as long as they are able. But your job, my darling, is that of the secret keeper. And not just my secrets, but the secrets of the many, many women we have saved. The children. The families.

If you leave Bitter House, if you sell or move away, things could be uncovered. Bodies, of course, but evidence too. The tunnels, the secrets kept in the walls. There are things hidden in Bitter House that could hurt good people if they're ever found by the wrong people. Though I am gone and can't be hurt anymore, there are women still out there, still alive and well, who are counting on you to protect them.

If I'd given the house to Jenn, she would've sold it. Without question. We've been offered ridiculous amounts of money to sell the house and land to developers, but doing so would have devastating results. This house in anyone else's hands would be disastrous.

It has to be you. I hope it will be you, my B.

It is a lonely, brutal task, to be the secret keeper, but one that I trust you can do with the grace of a Bitter. Because that's what you are, Bridget. That's what you will always be, regardless of the choice you make today. And I've left you in the good hands of Cole so you won't be alone. I suppose you could say I'm playing matchmaker, if you want to indulge me, but the truth is, I understand better than anyone how isolating this job can be. I did it alone for many years, even surrounded by my dearest friends.

I don't want that for you. I want you to love and be loved, Bridget, and even if that's not in the cards for the two of you, I like the idea of having someone around to protect you like he always protected me.

I am sorry for everything I ever did to hurt you. I hope you can understand why I made the choices I did, why I thought I was protecting you, though I'd never be so bold as to ask for your forgiveness. You don't owe me your forgiveness, darling. Or your understanding. Or your love, but you have always had mine.

Bitter House is yours now. Both of yours.

Take care of her and take care of yourselves. And if you ever decide to do what I have done, to spend your lives protecting others, the girls will show you the ropes. Keep my garden beautiful for me, will you?

I love you, my darling.

Yours forever,
Your grandmother
Vera Evelyn Bitter

P.S. There is a logbook in a vent in the ceiling of my closet. Please give it to Jane for safekeeping if you don't wish to have it. They will protect you with everything they have. None of this will fall on you should you choose to walk away. It will always be your choice.

When I stop reading, it takes me several seconds to look up. My vision is blurred with tears, the page now sprinkled with teardrops. When I meet the eyes of the women before me, I have no idea what to say.

"Your grandmother was a hero," Jane says, leaning forward over her knees. Something in her words snaps in my brain, and suddenly, I remember why I know her name. *Jane from the newspaper.*

"You wrote Vera's obituary."

She nods, tears filling her own eyes. The women on either side of her grasp her hands. "We knew she wouldn't have family to do it, and we understood why, but we couldn't let her pass away without honoring her in the only way we could. She was selfless, Bridget. And kind. She wanted to make the world better in the only way she knew how. And she deserved to have that truth out there for the world, even if they couldn't know the whole truth."

Cole slides his hand into mine, lacing our fingers together. For the first time in my entire life, I feel like I understand my grandmother. Maybe I don't agree with the way she handled things, but I do understand why she did it. And, if she hadn't, this man sitting next to me, the man who has protected me and stood up for me in ways I never knew about for my whole life, might not be here.

Vera was a lot of things—complicated and confusing and cold—but she was also a hero. She saved and protected and healed women and children in ways I will never know about. If that isn't using your power for the right causes, I'm not sure I know what is.

"We'll stay," I manage to choke out. "At Bitter House. I want to stay." I glance over at Cole, who nods, his dark eyes locking with mine in a way that tells me he's with me no matter what. That we're in this together, just like we've always been.

"Absolutely."

All three women give us knowing smiles, as if they never expected any different. And maybe they didn't. I have no idea if I want to be involved in any of this. But what I do know is that I will protect Bitter House's secrets with my life.

I'm a Bitter, after all. It's my legacy.

CHAPTER THIRTY-ONE

TEN YEARS LATER

When I answer the door, the woman is wearing a turtleneck sweater, hiding behind her husband. He's tall and charming, as they so often are. He smiles and holds his hand out, introducing himself as Dr. Martin.

I politely take his hand and step back, allowing him inside.

Jane and Cate are waiting in the living room to talk to him all about his growing practice, fluff his ego, and distract him, while Lily asks what his drink of choice is, and I pull his wife away to help her toward the tunnels. If she leaves now, she can make it into town in time to create an alibi.

Lily is in the kitchen when I return, sorting through the various dried petals we've collected from Vera's flower garden. She knows all about which ones do what thing, and she's slowly teaching me.

They're getting older, something that's undeniable. Someday, they'll be gone, too, and this will be all I have left of them. Their names, their legacies, their knowledge, their stories.

It won't get to be told, passed down through generations like it should, because their work isn't the kind you brag about. It's the kind that's necessary. Important. But done only in secret.

Cole comes into the room, giving us a warning that the women are on their way while Lily stirs Dr. Martin's glass of bourbon and passes it to me. When he enters the room, I hand him the tumbler before taking my wineglass from Cole.

Though Edna never wanted us to be involved in this side of the Bitter House legacy, Cole was the one who initially brought it up. In a way, he sees it as making up for the bad that his father did. Erasing it from his DNA somehow, covering up the stain.

Edna stays out of it, though I know it bothers her. She loves us just as she always has and just as she loved Vera, but she's not cut out for this part of what we do. It's too hard for her.

Still, I've gotten my wish. Though I didn't get the family I hoped for—we haven't spoken to Jenn or Zach since their legal battle over the will ended uneventfully—I managed to form a family of my own.

That's what we are: Cole, Jane, Cate, Lily, Edna, and me. Family dinners, holidays and all.

"Where's my wife?" Dr. Martin asks, his voice full of possession. She's not a person to him, but something to own. To claim.

"Bathroom," I mutter.

His lips press into a hard line, and I can tell he's not happy, but Cole distracts him again, asking about the sports car in the driveway. By dinner, the man is telling us all about his latest bid for mayor, and Lily has promised to make a big donation to his campaign.

It doesn't take long before he starts looking sleepy, though it's longer than we'd prefer. He's very boring, and the conversation is well past dragging at this point. When he goes down, we do a bit of a silent cheer, both because he'll never hurt anyone else, but also because we'll never have to hear him overuse the word *ambience* again.

Every time is a little bit different, but it's worth it. Maybe it's not right, like Vera said, but it's necessary. A lot has changed from the days when Vera wrote those first entries, but so much hasn't. Women still aren't protected like we should be. Men are given pass after pass, and women are given slips of paper for protection that mean nothing. Women have to prove everything while men are given the benefit of the doubt. If we speak up, it could ruin their lives, and they're *such nice guys*, so why would we do that?

Instead, we hold our keys between our fingers, walk faster or take another way home, send our location to friends from the back of a rideshare, or grit our teeth and bear it while another sexist remark is made by our boss or another scene of senseless cruelty is shown on television. Because if we don't, we're part of the problem. We're uptight. We can't take a joke.

It's not all men, I know, but it is all women. A collective

of shared experience, of intuition, of whispered warnings and knowing looks.

Don't get me wrong, I know there are nice guys left because I have one. I reach over and squeeze his hand under the table, so thankful for Vera, who saw what I couldn't all those years ago.

That night, when we're climbing into bed, bodies and palms sore and raw from digging yet another grave, I catch myself pausing when I spot a glimpse of my reflection in the mirror. I do that more and more these days.

Perhaps it's the silver that's starting to highlight my blonde hair, or maybe the delicate wrinkles near my eyes, but either way, as the years pass, I find it impossible to miss the resemblance to my grandmother.

She was beautiful, it's undeniable, but now I see the strength I always wrote off as coldness. The determination that always felt callous.

I see her truth, her passion, and her heart in my own eyes, and I couldn't be more grateful for everything she's done for me.

As I slide my wedding ring off and place it on the night-stand, I check my phone and see a new text message from Ana with an updated photo of Teddy and Olivia. A smile crosses my lips as I reply, letting her know how much I miss them all and how I can't wait for their next visit.

When I ease back onto the bed, my hand slips into Cole's. He squeezes it gently, massaging my tired muscles, and I smile to myself again.

Vera might've been stubborn, but these days, that feels

less like a flaw and more like a superpower. I hope someday I'm half the woman she was. That I'll have been able to help half the women she saved.

The hidden logbook is full of countless names, pages and pages of reasons for each death written in Vera's unmistakable hand. In her journal, she said she wanted to leave a legacy, and she has. The kind of legacy only the most stubborn, powerful woman could leave.

I release a long, peaceful sigh, settling in as Bitter House quiets all around us, keeping us safe and warm. As I close my eyes, Cole places one final kiss on my lips, pulling me into his chest, and I can't help thinking this house has never felt more like a home.

WOULD YOU RECOMMEND BITTER HOUSE?

If you enjoyed this story, please consider leaving me a quick review. It doesn't have to be long—just a few words will do. Who knows? Your review might be the thing that encourages a future reader to take a chance on my work! To leave a review, please visit: kierstenmodglinauthor.com/bitterhouse

Let everyone know how much you loved *Bitter House* on Goodreads: https://bit.ly/bitterhouse

STAY UP TO DATE ON EVERYTHING KMOD!

Thank you so much for reading this story. I'd love to invite you to sign up for my mailing list and text alerts so we can be sure you don't miss my next release.
Sign up for my mailing list here:
kierstenmodglinauthor.com/nlsignup

Sign up for my text alerts here:
kierstenmodglinauthor.com/textalerts

ACKNOWLEDGMENTS

As you probably know by now, I'm fascinated by the idea of home. So many of my stories feature characters who are either returning home or running from home (sometimes both). So when I decided to write this book, a story of a woman returning to the home she grew up in to learn secrets about the person who raised her, I knew I wanted to explore something deeper. Trust, home, and family are all things I explore often, and I wanted this story to go a bit further. Still, when I write my stories, even when they're fully plotted before I type the first word, I never really know what they're about until the end. As I began writing, so many themes came to me, like justice, being a woman in the world today, friendship, being let down by those around you, perception versus reality, and the idea of grieving over a relationship that was never what you thought it should be.

Like Bridget, I think many of us (myself included) know the pain of grieving a relationship over what you wish it was, while knowing it will never be that. Of wishing the person was someone they aren't. In Bridget's situation, that pain was amplified by knowing her relationship with Vera couldn't change because she'd passed away. When we lose the people in our lives, there are so many conflicted emotions involved, included regret. I think for so many of us, there will always be the wonder of how things might've been different if _____. So as I finished my first draft, I knew that was the story I wanted to tell in *Bitter House*. A story of loss and grief, justice and hope, a story of choices, but most importantly, a story that looks different depending on whose lens you're viewing it from.

Looking back on the past, you'll see very different stories from each of the characters' eyes, which of course describes life so well in general. Everyone keeps secrets, everyone wears masks, and everyone makes choices every single day that affect those around them. With *Bitter House*, I wanted to take a magnifying glass to that truth and examine it up close.

I wanted to look directly at the choices we make, the decisions we justify, and the people we hold close. At the end of the day, and at the end of my stories that is what life is about.

The choices, the people, and the ways we get through our days.

So, here's to my favorite choices, my best people, and my favorite souls to spend the day with:

To my husband and daughter—I love you both so much. Thank you for being the best parts of my day. Thank you for cheering me on, celebrating with me, and making the baby steps and giant leaps feel equally amazing. I couldn't do it without you two, and I wouldn't *want to*.

To my incredible editor, Sarah West—thank you for always seeing the story through the dusty piles of plot twists I hand you. I'm so grateful to have you on my team and to have built such a legacy with you. Thank you for everything you do for me.

To the awesome proofreading team at My Brother's Editor —thank you for being my final set of eyes and making sure everything shines!

To my loyal readers (AKA the #KMod Squad)—thank you for being in my corner every step of the way. Stories have always been my safe space, and the place I'd go when nothing else made sense about my world. I've spent all my life dreaming and hoping and wishing that someday, someone might want to read my ideas, listen to my characters, and live within my worlds for a few hours. When I started this journey, I wished for you. But in all of my wildest daydreams, I could've never imagined how amazing you'd be. Thank you for coming through for me, showing up for me, and cheering me on time and time again, story after story. I could never thank you enough for all you've done for me, but I will spend my life trying.

To my book club/gang/besties—thank you for everything you do for me. I'm so grateful for the laughs, inside jokes, tears, weekly venting sessions, and girls' trips. I love you all so much!

To my bestie, Emerald O'Brien—thank you for being the first set of eyes on every story and for cheering me along every step of the way! I'm so grateful for your friendship.

To my agent, Carly, and my audiobook publishing team at Dreamscape—thank you helping get my stories in front of as many readers as possible! I love our team!

Last but certainly not least, to you, dear reader—thank

you for taking a chance on this story, and on my art. There are countless stories out there begging for your attention, so the fact that you chose this one means the absolute world. I'm so grateful to get to go on these adventures with you and I hope this won't be our only one! I truly hope you loved Bridget's story. Thank you for trusting me to tell it. As always, whether this was your first Kiersten Modglin book or your 45th, I hope this journey was everything you hoped for and nothing like you expected.

ABOUT THE AUTHOR

KIERSTEN MODGLIN is a #1 bestselling author of psychological thrillers. Her books have sold over 1.5 million copies and been translated into multiple languages. Kiersten is a member of International Thriller Writers, Novelists, Inc., and the Alliance of Independent Authors. She is a KDP Select All-Star and a recipient of *ThrillerFix's* Best Psychological Thriller Award, *Suspense Magazine's* Best Book of 2021 Award, a 2022 Silver Falchion for Best Suspense, and a 2022 Silver Falchion for Best Overall Book of 2021. Kiersten grew up in rural western Kentucky and later relocated to Nashville, Tennessee, where she now lives with her family. Kiersten's readers across the world lovingly refer to her as "KMod." A binge-watching expert, psychology fanatic, and *indoor* enthusiast, Kiersten enjoys rainy days spent with her favorite people and evenings with her nose in a book.

Sign up for Kiersten's newsletter here:
kierstenmodglinauthor.com/nlsignup

Sign up for text alerts from Kiersten here:
kierstenmodglinauthor.com/textalerts

kierstenmodglinauthor.com
www.facebook.com/kierstenmodglinauthor
www.facebook.com/groups/kmodsquad
www.threads.net/kierstenmodglinauthor
www.instagram.com/kierstenmodglinauthor
www.tiktok.com/@kierstenmodglinauthor
www.goodreads.com/kierstenmodglinauthor
www.bookbub.com/authors/kiersten-modglin

ALSO BY KIERSTEN MODGLIN

STANDALONE NOVELS

Becoming Mrs. Abbott

The List

The Missing Piece

Playing Jenna

The Beginning After

The Better Choice

The Good Neighbors

The Lucky Ones

I Said Yes

The Mother-in-Law

The Dream Job

The Nanny's Secret

The Liar's Wife

My Husband's Secret

The Perfect Getaway

The Roommate

The Missing

Just Married

Our Little Secret

Widow Falls

Missing Daughter

The Reunion

Tell Me the Truth

The Dinner Guests

If You're Reading This...

A Quiet Retreat

The Family Secret

Don't Go Down There

Wait for Dark

You Can Trust Me

Hemlock

Do Not Open

You'll Never Know I'm Here

The Stranger

The Hollow

Bitter House

ARRANGEMENT TRILOGY

The Arrangement (Book 1)

The Amendment (Book 2)

The Atonement (Book 3)

THE MESSES SERIES

The Cleaner (Book 1)

The Healer (Book 2)

The Liar (Book 3)

The Prisoner (Book 4)

NOVELLAS

The Long Route: A Lover's Landing Novella

The Stranger in the Woods: A Crimson Falls Novella